PASSING

Nella Larsen

PASSING

Introduction by Ntozake Shange
Critical Foreword and Notes
by Mae Henderson

THE MODERN LIBRARY

NEW YORK

2002 Modern Library Paperback Edition

Biographical note copyright © 2000 by Random House, Inc.
Introduction copyright © 2000 by Ntozake Shange
Critical Foreword and notes copyright © 2002 by Mae Henderson
Reading group guide copyright © 2002 by
Random House, Inc.

LIBRARY OF CONGRESS CATALOGING-IN-PUBLICATION DATA
Larsen, Nella.
Passing/Nella Larsen ; introduction by Ntozake Shange ; critical
foreword and notes by Mae Henderson.—2002 Modern Library
pbk. ed.
p.   cm.
ISBN 0-375-75813-5
1. African American women—Fiction.
2. Passing (Identity)—Fiction.   3. Race relations—Fiction.
4. New York (N.Y.)—Fiction.   I. Title.
PS3523.A7225 P37   2002
813'.52—dc21   2001045037

Modern Library website address: www.modernlibrary.com

Printed in the United States of America

6   8   9   7   5

Nella Larsen

Nella Larsen, one of the most promising if enigmatic writers of the Harlem Renaissance, was born in Chicago of interracial parentage on April 13, 1891. Her father, who came from the Virgin Islands, died when she was two; her mother was of Danish origin. She grew up in a white world, primarily among people of German and Scandinavian stock. Her first experience with an all-black world occurred in 1909, when she matriculated at the high school division of Fisk University in Nashville, Tennessee. After studying at the University of Copenhagen for two years, Larsen moved to New York City in 1912 to study nursing at Lincoln Hospital. She later would train as a librarian, earning her certificate from the New York Public Library in 1923. In 1919 she married Elmer Samuel Imes, a prominent black research physicist, who introduced her to Harlem's literary and social elite. A job at the 135th Street branch of the New York Public Library brought her into contact with writers such as W.E.B. Du Bois, Countee Cullen, and Langston Hughes.

Larsen's first novel, *Quicksand,* was published by Knopf in 1928. The largely autobiographical story of a mulatto woman who searches in vain for sexual and racial identity, *Quicksand* was awarded a Bronze Medal by the Harmon Foundation in recognition of Distinguished Achievement Among Negroes in Literature. "This is an articulate, sympathetic first novel, which tells its story and projects its heroine in a lucid, unexaggerated manner," said *The New York Times Book Review.* W.E.B. Du Bois deemed *Quicksand* "a fine, thoughtful and courageous work ... the best piece of fiction that Negro America has produced since the heyday of [Charles] Chestnutt."

Passing, Larsen's tragic and remarkably candid story of a light-skinned black woman who chooses to "pass" as white for economic security and social status, was published by Knopf in 1929. Critic Robert Bone considered the novel "the best treatment of the subject in Negro fiction." The *Saturday Review* wrote: "Miss Larsen has produced a work so fine, sensitive, and distinguished that it rises above race categories and becomes that rare object, a good novel." And *The New York Times Book Review*, although critical of the novel's "suspiciously 'made' ending," praised Larsen's skillful tracing of "the involved processes of a mind divided against itself, that fights between the dictates of reason and desire. [Larsen] follows the windings of Irene Redfield's thought without chasing the fleeting shades of cerebral processes into blind alleys."

In 1930 Larsen became the first African American woman to be awarded a Guggenheim Fellowship in creative writing, but her personal life and career as a novelist suffered several reversals during the early years of the Depression. Erroneously accused of plagiarizing the short story "Sanctuary," which appeared in *Forum* magazine under her name, she was unable to have a third novel accepted for publication. Following a highly publicized divorce in 1933, Larsen gradually withdrew from literary circles and abandoned writing altogether. She spent the last twenty years of her life working as a nurse in Manhattan hospitals. Nella Larsen died in New York City on March 30, 1964.

"Nella Larsen had no peer among Harlem Renaissance writers in the kinds of questions she posed in her novels," judged Thadious M. Davis, Larsen's biographer. Mary Helen Washington, writing in *Ms.* magazine, claimed, "The women in her novels, like Larsen, are driven to emotional and psychological extremes in their attempts to handle ambivalence, marginality, racism, and sexism. She has shown us that behind the carefully manicured exterior, behind the appearance of security is a woman who hears the beating of her wings against a walled prison." Alice Walker concurred: "*Quicksand* and *Passing* are novels I will never forget. They open up a whole world of experience and struggle that seemed to me, when I first read them years ago, absolutely absorbing, fascinating, and indispensable."

CONTENTS

INTRODUCTION

Ntozake Shange

As a person of color—light brown by most standards, but not light enough to pass—I've often wondered about the lives of childhood friends and family members who took that precipitous step and crossed over the color line to become white. Remembering that I am of a generation that straddled the era of strict segregation of the races and the toppling of that abominable separation of black and white, I've experienced the denigration that Clare Kendry, Nella Larsen's protagonist in *Passing,* sought to escape. So I understand the impulse not to announce to everyone that which they can't ascertain on their own. Or as Larsen writes:

Absurd! Impossible! White people were so stupid about such things for all that they usually asserted that they were able to tell; and by the most ridiculous means finger-nails, palms of hands, shapes of ears, teeth, and other equally silly rot. They always took her for an Italian, a Spaniard, a Mexican, or a gipsy. Never, when she was alone, had they even remotely seemed to suspect that she was a Negro.

Clare Kendry, unlike her friend Irene Redfield, takes it upon herself to pass. But the aloneness brings her back time and again to the lives of certain of her old school friends, people who know she is a Negro but who are as capable of passing as she is. It is as if Larsen wanted to invite us into a closed circle of the well-off light-skinned Negroes who distance themselves from their darker brethren by class, color, and fashion.

It is impossible to escape the beauty of Clare Kendry, her sense of fashion and drawing room manners. As Larsen writes:

Clare, exquisite, golden, fragrant, flaunting, in a stately gown of shining black taffeta, whose long, full skirt lay in graceful folds about her slim golden feet; her glistening hair drawn smoothly back into a small twist at the nape of her neck; her eyes sparkling like dark jewels.

At one point Irene Redfield thinks that Clare was born out of her correct era, that she belongs in the time of French salons and the antebellum South—which is telling, because both of these epochs were sustained by the exploitation of the masses of people. Irene, too, is seduced by Clare's beauty, her mystery, and brazen risk taking. For Clare is married to a man who literally hates Negroes and doesn't know he is married to one—he calls her "Nig" as a private joke for how dark she got in the sun.

And Clare wants Irene to provide her entrée into the Negro society of the 1920s, though she could lose everything: someone might see her and put two and two together. (If you socialize with Negroes, you must be one—who else but "colored" would want to be around us?)

Clare wants Irene to lay her life open to her on a whim—on the occasion of her husband's absence, whenever it pleases her to visit the "Negro," as if Irene were there for her amusement, to see Negroes, not unlike the hordes of whites who invaded Harlem at the time to look at us, to dance our dances, to guess who among us was more white than the others. Irene realizes that "Clare Kendry cared nothing for the race. She only belonged to it."

This sort of betrayal tortured Irene, as does her

husband's friendliness toward Clare. Brian Redfield is a handsome and accomplished doctor. He longed for some of the freedoms his color denied him, and his true private obsession is Brazil, where, he imagines, color is of no import. Irene insists he give up the fantasy of Brazil for her sake, their children's, and their comfortable life. She refuses to take his dream seriously.

Irene is tormented by both these forces—Clare Kendry's passing back and forth and Brian Redfield's resentment that she is the cause of his lack of freedom. Irene cherishes her boys of different colors and her secure life during Harlem's Renaissance as a member of the elite light-skinned Talented Tenth. She takes pride in the advancement of the race, as evidenced by her participation in the Negro Welfare League—though her husband sees it as an unwelcome obligation to help the poorer brothers. Let there be no mistake, Larsen bluntly exposes the classism and racism of this small clique of our population by offering no personalities for the household help of the Redfield house: black and poor and ignored except for their efficiency. So, Irene Redfield's suffering brought about by Clare Kendry is limited to the fate of her class and caste. Irene even upbraids her husband for speaking honestly about lynchings because she wants her sons to be "happy," meaning ignorant of the true perils of Negro life at that time.

Nevertheless, Irene Redfield openly participates in Clare Kendry's very dangerous tiptoeing back and forth over the color line and guards Clare Kendry's charade like an obsessed lover, constantly submitting herself to the allure of Clare's beauty and the "furtive mystery" of her person. There is no way to ignore the homoerotic undertones of their relationship, as evidenced in one of Clare Kendry's letters to Irene:

> ... For I am so lonely ... cannot help longing to be with you again, as I have never longed for anything before; and I have wanted many things in my life. ... You can't know how in this pale life of mine I am all the time seeing the bright pictures of that other that I once thought I was glad to be free of. ... It's like an ache, a pain that never ceases. ...

In kind Irene Redfield suffers fits of depression and teary bouts of guilt about her relationship with Clare to the point that she becomes jealous of her husband's very innocent relationship with her friend.

In this exquisitely written volume, Nella Larsen has peeled away the historical questions we might have about society during the Harlem Renaissance, while remaining relevant in an America whose biracial population is growing. She offers characters so honest and desperate to be whole that we cannot help but champion their humanity.

———

NTOZAKE SHANGE is a renowned playwright (*for colored girls who have considered suicide / when the rainbow is enuf*), poet (*Nappy Edges* and *The Love Space Demands*), and novelist (*Betsey Brown; Liliane;* and *Sassafrass, Cypress & Indigo*). She lives in Texas with her daughter.

CRITICAL FOREWORD

Mae G. Henderson

Like other novels of the Harlem Renaissance, Nella Larsen's *Passing* (1929) has been read in terms of African American modernism, a term linking the aesthetic and political dimensions of this outpouring of work by black artists in the 1920s, and designating literary techniques ranging from the experimentalism of Jean Toomer to the realism of Rudolph Fisher to the romantic racialism of Claude McKay. In *Passing,* as in other novels of the Harlem School, the city—particularly Harlem—functions as a kind of topos that becomes a site of transformation and, potentially, liberation in that decade of black cultural and social awakening.[1] Although the opening scene of what

Larsen calls the "Encounter" between her two main characters occurs in their native Chicago, the main action and denouement of the novel transpires in New York, the mecca of the "New Negro" and locus of the "New Woman." The geographical location of Larsen's characters in Chicago and New York codes the "city" as both a space of ethnic and social diversity in the aftermath of the Great Migration, as well as a space newly open to the "feminine" during an era when women were moving from the domestic sphere into the public culture. Larsen's self-conscious engagement with an urban culture of modernity from which her characters derive their location of social marginality—as blacks and women—is particularly pertinent to the narrative theme of racial passing, since, as critic Werner Sollors aptly notes, a primary condition of passing in the United States has been "social and geographical mobility," especially as it prevails "in environments such as cities . . . that provided anonymity to individuals, permitting them to resort to imaginative role-playing in their self-representation."[2] Situated during an era of profound cultural change and social transition, Larsen's modern passing characters distinctly "belong to [their] own time," in that these "raced" and "gendered" subjects inhabit a social geography that both affirms and contests social, economic, and political arrangements that sustain the "color line" demarcating race and the "separate spheres" defining gender.

As one of several (albeit only two women) novelists of the period, Larsen is distinctive in that her novels, unlike those of Renaissance writers such as Jessie Fauset, Walter White, Claude McKay, Rudolph Fisher, and Wallace Thurman, not only engage the racial thematics of African American modernism but also deploy the formal techniques of Anglo-American and European modernism. Larsen's modernist articulations, mediated from the perspectives of race, gender, and sexuality, are demonstrated by what Rita Felski defines in *The Gender of Modernity* as "aesthetic self-consciousness, stylistic fragmentation, and . . . questioning of representation" within the context of "a distinctively modern sense of dislocation and ambiguity."[3] In addition, Larsen's figuration of the African American woman as a racially marked, middle-class, gendered subject in both her first novel, *Quicksand* (1928), and her second, *Passing,* privilege the mulatto, or biracial, woman in particular as the site of contradiction and negotiation, transgression and conformity, tradition and modernity. In some respects, the complexity of this image, as we shall see, marks this figure as a signifier—a duplicitous signifier—of the competing impulses, ideologies, and aesthetics characterizing the Harlem Renaissance itself.

But Larsen's latter novel also belongs to a genre, the passing narrative, that some critics maintain has become defunct. Surely it is true, as some have argued, that "passing," in the sense of "passing for white," has ceased to be the social issue that it was in the nineteenth and early twentieth centuries,[4] yet the recent republication of Larsen's novel, along with James Weldon Johnson's *Autobiography of an Ex-Colored Man,* would suggest that perhaps W.E.B. Du Bois was not entirely accurate in his prediction that the "intriguing and ticklish subject" of passing "is all a pretty, silly matter of no real importance which another generation will comprehend with great difficulty."[5] And while, as Gayle Wald has documented, the postwar 1950s witnessed the emergence of what she describes as the "postpassing" narrative in black popular fiction, it is demonstrably evident that this genre has discovered a receptive audience during the latter part of the twentieth and early twenty-first centuries.[6] Much of the renewed interest in this genre is, of course, due to the emergence of an increased interest in what Werner Sollors has defined as a tradition of "interracial literature" as well as in a more general preoccupation with notions of hybridity, biraciality, and social constructionism as they structure contemporary conceptions of personal and social identity.

Although *Quicksand* has traditionally received the higher critical regard, it would seem that in light of recent attention, a reevaluation of *Passing* is due. Arguing that Larsen's craft and subtlety demand an acknowledgment of the status of *Passing* as a major novel of the Harlem Renaissance, contemporary critics have insisted on according Larsen's novel its "rightful place" in the canons of American, African American, and women's literature.[7] Historically, however, Larsen's reputation rests less on *Passing* than on her first novel, *Quicksand*. In a contemporary review of *Quicksand* in *The Crisis,* W.E.B. Du Bois pronounced it a "fine, thoughtful and courageous piece of work," the best that "Negro America has produced since the heyday of Charles Chesnutt."[8] And although Du Bois praised Larsen's second novel as "one of the finest novels of the year," *Passing* has not always fared so well among later critics and scholars.[9] While rating *Passing* as "probably the best treatment of the subject [of passing] in Negro fiction," critic Robert

Bone considers it Larsen's "less important novel."[10] Comparing it to the typical "women's magazine story," Hoyt Fuller describes *Passing* as a "flawed" and "rather banal" novel."[11] Hiroko Sato describes *Passing* as a "slight book," written by a novelist who wrote "only one good book [*Quicksand*]."[12] Nathan Irvin Huggins ranks *Quicksand* as Larsen's "best novel," and *Passing* her "lesser novel."[13] David Levering Lewis views *Quicksand* as "one of the . . . best novels of the Renaissance,"[14] and George Hutchinson regards it as "the best novel of the Harlem Renaissance until Zora Neale Hurston's *Their Eyes Were Watching God*."[15] Cheryl Wall comments on the "inevitable melodrama," that "weakens the credibility" of Larsen's second novel."[16] And one of Larsen's biographers, Charles Larson, suggests that "*Passing* is a lesser novel than *Quicksand*," while another biographer, Thadious Davis, considers it "less skillfully developed," although "more carefully structured" than her first novel.[17]

Despite these evaluations, *Passing* has established itself during the last two decades or so as a major work of the Harlem Renaissance as well as an important contribution to the genre known as the "modernist passing narrative." What is less well known is that the novel also belongs to a literary pedigree that links the narrative of passing to an originary form of African American literature. Genealogically, the narrative of passing traces its lineage back to the nineteenth-century African American slave narrative. Elements of the passing narrative can be found in several of the slave narratives, including *Running a Thousand Miles for Freedom; or the Escape of William and Ellen Craft from Slavery* (1860), in which two slaves successfully escape from bondage by having the light-skinned Ellen "pass" for the "white" (and male) master of her dark-skinned slave husband, William. Not only does "the passing plot"[18] appear in the narratives of the fugitive slave who sometimes deployed racial passing as a strategy by which to escape the fetters of slavery, it also resurfaces as a plot element in nineteenth-century African American fiction, including ex-slave author William Wells Brown's *Clotel, A Tale of the Southern States* (1864)[19]; Frank J. Webb's *The Garies and Their Friends* (1857); Francis Ellen Watkins Harper's *Iola Leroy* (1892); as well as Hannah Craft's recently "discovered" *The Bondwoman's Narrative* (c. 1853–60), now deemed to be the earliest novel by a black woman in the United States.[20] Richard Hildreth's *The Slave; or, Memoirs of Archy Moore* (1836) and

Harriet Beecher Stowe's *Uncle Tom's Cabin* (1852), both Anglo-American novels modeled on the narratives of ex-slaves, also deploy the passing plot.[21]

The recurrence of the passing plot in both black and white fiction in the United States would suggest the importance of passing as a social issue from the late nineteenth well into the twentieth century. Indeed, two years following the publication of Larsen's novel, one Caleb Johnson wrote in the *Outlook and Independent* that "crossing the color line is so common an occurrence that the Negroes have their own well-understood word for it. They call it 'passing.' "[22] Writing in *The Saturday Review of Literature* in 1947, Walter White, himself a "voluntary Negro," observed, "Every year approximately 12,000 white-skinned Negroes disappear—people whose absence cannot be explained by death or emigration ... men and women who have decided that they will be happier and more successful if they flee from the proscription and humiliation which the American color line imposes on them."[23] Clearly, White's statistics regarding the occurrence and extent of race passing in the United States must be viewed as highly speculative, since evidence supporting such claims, by its very nature, remains scant and anecdotal due to the conditions of secrecy upon which the success of the racial passer is predicated.

Further commenting on the theme of passing in the literature of black and white Americans, Swedish sociologist Gunnar Myrdal also notes the conditions of secrecy and silence that alone guarantee the success of the racial passer, whom he identifies, broadly speaking, as "a Negro [who] becomes a white man ... [who] moves from the lower to the higher caste." Passing can be secured, explains Myrdal, "only by the deception of the white people with whom the passer comes to associate and by a conspiracy of silence on the part of other Negroes who might know about it." Myrdal describes the typical passing plot and its reception:

> As a social phenomenon, passing is so deeply connected with the psychological complexes—built around caste and sex—of both groups that it has come to be a central theme of fiction and of popular imagination and story telling. The adventures of the lonesome passer, who extinguishes his entire earlier life, breaks all personal and social anchorings, and starts a new life where he has to fear his own shadow, are alluring to all and have an espe-

cially frightening import to whites. There is a general sentimentality for the unhappy mulatto—the "marginal man" with split allegiances and frustrations in both directions which is especially applied to the mulatto who passes.[24]

Although like Myrdal, African American critic Sterling Brown emphasizes the "unhappiness" or "wretchedness" of the passing subject, Brown further distinguishes between black- and white-authored treatments of the passing subject during the Harlem Renaissance:

> We have seen that the mulatto who "passes" has been a victim of opposing interpretations. Negro novelists urge his unhappiness, until he is summoned back to his people by the spirituals, or their full-throated laughter, or their simple ways. . . . White novelists insist upon the mulatto's unhappiness for other reasons. To them he is the anguished victim of a divided inheritance. Mathematically they work it out that his intellectual strivings and self-control come from his white blood, and his emotional urgings, indolence and potential savagery come from his Negro blood. Their favorite character, the octoroon, wretched because of the

"single drop of midnight in her veins," desires a white lover above all else, and must therefore go down to a tragic end.[25]

Both Myrdal and Brown emphasize the psychic alienation and social dislocation inhabited by the literary passing subject who is compelled to maintain a position of "disidentification"[26] relative to both the dominant oppressive culture and the dominated oppressed culture. And despite arguments to the contrary, Brown's distinction between popular black- and white-authored representations of the mixed-race subject would seem to be not entirely without justification, especially as it informs the conventional physical, moral, and intellectual ascriptions attached to race in nineteenth-century American literature.

Notably, the popularity of the passing genre before and after the 1920s is attested not only in African American fiction such as Charles W. Chesnutt's *The House Behind the Cedars* (1900) and his recently recovered *Paul Marchand, F.M.C.* (c. 1920), James Weldon Johnson's *Autobiography of an Ex-Colored Man* (1912; 1927), Walter White's *Flight* (1926), Jessie Fauset's *Plum Bun* (1928), George Schuyler's *Black No More* (1931), and Nella Larsen's *Passing,* but also by Anglo-American fiction such as Rebecca Hard-ing Davis's *Waiting for the Verdict* (1867), William Dean Howells's *An Imperative Duty* (1892), and Mark Twain's *Pudd'nhead Wilson* (1894). Elements of the passing plot also appear in Harriet Beecher Stowe's *Uncle Tom's Cabin* (1852) and William Faulkner's *Light in August* (1932) and *Absalom, Absalom!* (1936). Later treatments of the passing plot range from Fannie Hurst's popular *Imitation of Life* (1933; made into a movie in 1959) to Danzy Senna's more recent *Caucasia* (1998) along with Philip Roth's *The Human Stain* (2000).

Contemporary critics have not only noted the popularity of the passing plot, especially during the Harlem Renaissance, but have further emphasized the social and political function of the passing narrative. Commenting on the irony of passing as a "major theme of the 1920s when race pride was supposedly at a peak," feminist critic Barbara Christian argues that this form, in fact, "heightened the white audience's awareness of the restrictions imposed upon talented blacks who then found it necessary to become white in order to fulfill themselves." Christian also observes that in the African American version of the passing novel, "the passer is often a woman who believes that through marriage to a wealthy white man, she might gain economic security and more freedom of mobility."[27] Christian's particular focus on the role of the "*mulatta*," and the significance of gender, sex, and marriage in a domestic plot enframed by a larger social narrative of patriarchy, as we shall see, would constitute key elements of feminist analysis by contemporary critics of Nella Larsen's *Passing*.

Locating the "passing" novel within his cultural and political narrative of nationalism and assimilation, critic Robert Bone defines the "attack upon passing" by the "Rear Guard" of the Harlem Renaissance as an "affirmation of race loyalty," and thus a "manifestation of . . . nationalism." Bone argues that "if the act of passing is an expression of assimilation carried to its logical conclusion, then surely a novel which condemns passing must have nationalist implications." For Bone, then, the passing novel represents, "in psychological terms, a symbolic rejection of the author's unconscious desire to be white"—a fictional projection whose repudiation "fortifies . . . racial loyalty against the threat from within."[28]

On the other hand, Amritjit Singh maintains that the appearance of so many passing novels during the twenties is "evidence of [the] predominantly middle-class orientation" of the Harlem Renaissance novelists. In support of this class narrative, Singh cites

Claude McKay's claim in *Banjo* (1929) that "passing white" was a "common [topic] of colored intelligentsia" but had little meaning or relevance for lower-class blacks. Explaining the attraction of the modernist passing novel for Harlem Renaissance writers, Singh observes the double move of this genre: "[A]t one level there is an attempt to delineate a dimension of culture and values which the middle class shared with the white American. At the same time, these novels inform white readers that middle-class blacks have no intention or desire to relinquish the joy and abandon of black life for the dullness of the white bourgeoisie."[29] What Singh identifies here is a contradictory narrative impulse that negotiates between an ideology of universalism at the level of national culture and an ethos of particularism at the level of lived racial experience.

Not only do Bone and Singh affirm the logic of racial difference implicit in passing, but both emphasize the passing novel's narrative trajectory as one of return, or "homecoming," deriving from a sense of the subject's racial allegiance and/or affinity. What is less clear in their analyses, but more evident in the novels, is that it is precisely the social construction of identity, often due to advantages of class and culture, that allows the passing subject to cross into

the "white" world, while a more essentialist notion
of identity, based on atavistic "yearnings" or racial
fealty, inevitably returns this character to the racial
fold. Thus, while the logic of passing would seem, on
the one hand, to subvert the logic of racial difference,
it seems, on the other, paradoxically, to affirm a racial
or cultural essence that has the effect of naturaliz-
ing difference. Not unlike other narratives of passing,
Larsen's novel, as we shall see, expresses this tension
between social constructionism and the competing
narrative of essentialism that has engaged postmodern discourse.

Although the passing novel, as suggested above,
enables some writers to emphasize the uniqueness
and particularity of black culture, most black writers
also represent passing as a strategy that interrogates
the color line and the entitlements attached to whiteness as a marker of social status and economic privilege. While Anglo-American writers who treat these
issues (e.g., Stowe, Twain, Faulkner) both critique and
at times narratively reproduce the racial (and sometimes racist) arrangements and practices inscribed in
the legal fiction and social custom of racial classification codified in court decisions such as *Plessy vs.
Ferguson* (1896), African American writers have historically deployed passing and the passing subject as

narrative devices by which to critique racist and hier-archal social structures and practices while, at the same time, promoting the value of blackness.

It has by now been amply demonstrated that the modern African American novel as a genre owes a great debt, formally and thematically, to the slave narrative. What is not so frequently acknowledged is that this genre is similarly indebted to the passing narrative, arguably the successor to the slave narra-tive as the most identifiable black literary form of the early twentieth century. And while never as popular as the slave narrative, the narrative of passing in-scribes several of the same themes and motifs as its more illustrious predecessor. The passing narratives contest and constitute part of the critique of race and racial difference that is first formally articulated in the slave narratives. Like the slave narrative, it is a genre that is both political and moral in its appeal to the reader. If the slave narrative functions as a cri-tique of slavery (and to some extent northern racism), the passing narrative functions as a critique of post-bellum social structures based on racial segregation, white privilege, and black subordination. And if the slave narrative articulates the fundamental humanity of blacks, the passing novel advances its claim to the civil equality of African Americans. Finally, the passing narrative, like the slave narrative, is a form that both explicitly and implicitly challenges hierarchical and discriminatory social, political, and economic practices.

Further, the narrative of slavery and the narrative of passing replicate certain formal and structural patterns: Structured by border crossings—social, personal, and sometimes literal—both can be classified as "border" narratives. If the slave narrator crosses the geographical border from South to North, the passing narrator transgresses the racial boundary from "black" to "white." If the slave crosses the Mason-Dixon line, the passer crosses the color line, the one in an attempt to secure physical freedom, the other to secure social freedom. More frequently, however, the passing protagonist reverses the slave's journey of geographical "leavetaking" to one of racial "homecoming"—psychically if not always physically.

Historically, the slave narrative and the passing narrative have appealed to both black and white writers, but these forms have also attracted both black and white readers. If it is true, as some critics maintain, that the slave narrative "educate[d] white America about its 'exotic' and unknown 'other,'" the passing narrative not only educated whites ethnographically about black life, it has constructed and critiqued "whiteness" for both its black and white readers.[30] While its exoticism offered whites a lens into an aspect of black life rarely witnessed by outsiders, its social critique locates the passing narrative within the tradition of protest and exposé that characterizes much of nineteenth- and early-twentieth-century black literary discourse.

Moreover, just as the slave narrative emerged as a countergenre to the southern "plantation tradition," so the narrative of passing arose in dialectical response to a body of postbellum literature seeking to reinscribe the color line in the popular literature of the period. Southern novelists like Thomas Dixon, Robert Lee Durham, and Thomas Nelson Page typically portrayed blacks, especially mulattoes, as "dangerous" and "threatening" to civilization and the southern way of life.[31] The passing narrative, on the other hand, often reveals the violence, brutality, and inhumanity of whites toward blacks, as well as the pathos of the mulatto's plight.

The passing narrative, like the slave narrative, emerges from a precise historical period and, as such, compels both readers and critics alike to take into account the social and cultural history that is formally inscribed in the genre. The motivation and investment in passing was a direct consequence of slavery and its aftermath, which legally defined race as an instrument to insure the social privilege and material property attached to "whiteness." As David Roediger demonstrates, to be white in the early and mid-nineteenth century meant to be "not black," and to be "not black" meant, as Ruth Frankenberg explains, to be "not slave."[32] (Thus, the idea of the "white slave" in the United States, as critic Werner Sollors notes, constituted a "cultural oxymoron."[33]) And finally, the mergence of race with social and legal status, as critical race theorist Cheryl Harris explains, marked the distinction between "who was subject to enslavement" and "who was free." Whiteness thus became a "valuable" and "valued" property, the "quintessential property for personhood," and "inherent in the concept of 'being white' was the right to own or hold whiteness to the exclusion and subordination of Blacks."[34] Thus, according to Harris, the social construction of race turns on the "ideological and rhetorical move from 'slave' to 'free' [and] 'Black' and 'white' as polar constructs—moves, I might add, to which the slave narrative and passing narrative implicitly respond."[35] Since stories of "passing" are, however, also stories of racial intermixing, these narratives threaten the ideology of (white) racial purity and privilege. In fact, it is the offspring of racial fusion, as Eva Saks notes, that "produced the phenomenon of 'passing' . . . for white" that is inscribed in the passing narrative."[36]

Fundamentally transgressive in ideology, the passing narratives not only explore the social, psychological, and economic motivations for passing, they also perform acts of literary trespass in exposing the cultural and legal fiction of race. *Plessy vs. Ferguson,* whose consequences can be ignored neither in the social institution of passing nor in the narrativization of that experience in the novel of passing, not only legally codified the color line, relegating blacks for the next half century to a status of "separate but equal," it also secured the "one drop" rule by which "blackness" was defined. In fact, it was this conception that race was biologically determined, and expressed through what Saks calls "the metaphor of blood," that not only instituted segregation in the form of Jim Crow laws, it also essentialized the notion of race in American jurisprudence. And it was this notion that the infusion of "one drop" of "black blood" was racially determinative that rendered what Joel Williamson describes as "invisible blackness."[37] In literature, it is the function of the passing subject, through whose veins supposedly flow the "contamination" of "black blood," to expose the fiction of race and racial classification as well as to represent the desire of all African Americans for full access to the rights and privileges of citizenship. As a form, then, the passing novel destabilizes social and personal identities, creating a fluidity and mobility that transgresses the boundaries of race inscribed by law and custom, and, at the same time, this genre denounces a social system based on racial hierarchy and exclusion.

Under the guise of genteel bourgeois domestic fiction, Larsen's passing plot enables the writer to interrogate notions frequently associated with the social sciences, or what subsequently became known as "scientific racism." And although *Passing* did not appear until the end of the third decade of the twentieth century, the novel engages an ongoing historical discourse of race and race difference that continued to inform the emergent "scientific" disciplines of sociology, anthropology, and ethnology, discourses advancing ideas of fundamental racial difference, often couched in notions of social Darwinism and evolutionism designed to provide a rationale for policies aimed at justifying an expanding U.S. imperialism as well as "resolving" what was popularly regarded on the home front as the "race problem."

Just as modern cultural anthropologists like Franz Boas and Melville Herskovits countered the racialist theories of nineteenth- and early-twentieth-century social science discourse, so Larsen's passing plot calls into question popular theories contrived to reify notions of race and race difference. Larsen's ironic appropriations and allusions to the discourses of miscegenation, genetics, heredity, eugenics, and genealogy engage popular Victorian pseudoscientific, legal, and religious theories of race and racial difference. Frequent sardonic allusions in Larsen's text to "Ham," "blood," "fingernails," and so forth, as well as narrative anxieties around issues of the body, color, and reproduction, reflect Larsen's interrogation of popular scriptural justifications of slavery as well as theories of scientific racialism popularized by Louis Agassiz, Josiah C. Nott, Sir Francis Galton,[38] and their successors, who sought—through arcane mathematical calculation, theories of mono- and polygenesis, phrenology, amalgamation, atavism, and so forth—to discover outward racial signs or markers designed to classify race and essentialize racial differences.

The passing plot itself turns centrally on the notions of personal and racial identity—and whether it is produced by biology and genetics (nature) or environment and training (culture). Like other black women novelists of the Harlem Renaissance, Larsen addresses in her fiction issues of gender, sexuality, and class as they intersect with race to produce the race-marked middle-class female subject. Further, as Cheryl Wall, Thadious Davis, Judith Butler, and others have argued, Larsen's treatment of the passing female subject and her social location draws on the notion of performative identity.[39] By rewriting modernist notions of a constative, immutable, unified notion of selfhood with a conception of identity that is fundamentally performative, the narrative of passing interrogates the idea of a transcendent or essentialized identity. Many contemporary theorists reject essentializing notions of identity that have been enlisted historically to justify and rationalize racial, gender, sexual, and national hierarchies whereby women, blacks, gays, and colonials have been subjugated. Nevertheless, in contemporary literary and theoretical discourse, the relation between essentialism and constructionism remains a site of critique and debate. As we shall see, Larsen, in effect, narratively theorizes the current postmodernist debate around essentialism vs. constructionism. And like some other narratives of passing, Larsen's plot betrays a certain duplicity in that it seems to challenge the idea of innate racial difference while, at the same time, making a case for racial uniqueness.

—

Critics have interpreted Larsen's title, and the trope of "passing" itself, in several different registers. For Mary Helen Washington, passing becomes "a metaphor for the risk-taking experience," as well as "a symbol or metaphor of deliverance," albeit it "an obscene form of deliverance," since it requires denial of roots and genealogy.[40] For Cheryl Wall, passing becomes "a metaphor of death and desperation," referring not only to "the sociological phenomenon of blacks crossing the color line," but also to "the racial identity and the denial of self required of women who conform to restrictive gender roles."[41] Deborah McDowell suggests that passing is a metaphor that implies "false, forged, and mistaken" racial, sexual, and narrative identities.[42] As these and other critics suggest, Larsen's title, functioning as the novel's central trope, would seem to refer ambiguously to both Irene Redfield and Clare Kendry, both of whom play the passing game—although for the former, the decision to pass is merely "occasional."

Despite the painstaking and illuminating work of Thadious Davis and Charles Larson, Nella Larsen remains, in many respects, what Mary Helen Washington once described as "mystery woman of the Harlem Renaissance."[43] The gaps and ambiguities in her biography are similarly reflected in her novel *Passing*, which remains, in some respects, the "mystery text" of the Harlem Renaissance.

Critical efforts to unmask Larsen's text have yielded multiple readings, ranging from a focus on race, to psychology, class, gender, (lesbian) sexuality, to an approach based on the intersectionality of many of these categories of analysis. Many critics, including Claudia Tate, Cheryl Wall, Mary Dearborn, Charles Larson, and Deborah McDowell, argue that Larsen deploys a cover story based on race to conceal a deeper, more complex narrative. For Tate, Larsen's narrative draws its power not "from its surface content [race], but from its vivid imagery, subtle metaphors, and carefully balanced psychological ambiguity." Viewing passing as "more a device to sustain suspense than merely a compelling social issue," Tate contends that "racial issues . . . are, at best, peripheral to the story."[44] Cheryl Wall argues that Larsen's text was subject to popular misreadings, concluding that "[r]eaders were so sure they knew the story Larsen was telling they misread the story she actually told." Larsen, in effect, deployed the convention of the tragic mulatto, argues Wall, to "mask her . . . subversive concerns . . . about gender questions."[45] Similarly, for Mary Dearborn, race functions only on the symbolic level, since "the problems Larsen's heroines suffer derive from their identities as women."[46] Each of the foregoing interpretations valorizes Larsen's text not for its engagement with issues of race and identity, but for its modernist aesthetics on the one hand, and its construction and critique of gender and gender ideology on the other.

Similar to critics before her, Deborah McDowell seeks to reveal a "dangerous subplot" underpinning a safer, more conventional surface story of race. In her influential reading, McDowell interprets Larsen's novel as a story of lesbian sexuality that "passes" itself off as a story of race: "Though superficially, Irene's is an account of Clare's passing for white and related to issues of racial identity and loyalty," maintains McDowell, "underneath the safety of that surface is the more dangerous story . . . of Irene's awakening sexual desire for Clare."[47] Charles Larson, too, maintains that "the racial theme" is not "the most important"; rather "the racial question . . . is the framework for Larsen's . . . novel, the context she used to develop her major theme of marital instability."[48] In thus overwriting the story of racial passing with a modernist aesthetics of form or an ideological reading of gender, sexuality, and domesticity, contemporary critics seek to revise and expand earlier, more traditional race readings. By relegating the story of race passing to the status of symbol or "cover" story, however, these critical accounts risk eclipsing or segregating race from other important elements of the narrative.

Contrary to many of the writers above, my own analysis will strategically recenter race in order to demonstrate precisely how Larsen's novel critiques and embraces the notion of race as an essentialist constuction. From a critical perspective, what seems clear, as Jennifer Brody and Ann duCille suggest, is that Larsen's simultaneous engagement with the interarticulations of race, class, gender, and sexuality ultimately produces a text whose horizon of meaning must inevitably exceed any univocal reading.[49]

—

Larsen takes as her subject middle-class black women who, like the author herself, often discover themselves marginalized by their mulatta, or biracial, status. And although most critics now agree that Larsen's novel reflects Irene Redfield's rather than Clare Kendry's story, Clare, like her creator, has remained something of an enigma for the reader. Yet Clare Kendry has little in common with earlier nineteenth-century portraits of the tragic mulatta. And while Clare as mulatta may indeed function as a "narrative device of mediation" (Hazel Carby) or "rhetorical device" (Ann duCille), Larsen refuses her character the sentimental incarnation of the tragic mulatta whose plight necessarily enlists the sympathy of the reader.[50] Further, unlike the mulatto characters of earlier abolitionist and black protest fiction, Clare is devoid of race consciousness, expressing neither commitment nor solidarity to race. (Rather, it is Irene who is identified as the "race woman" by virtue of her discourse on "race uplift."). Although humorously fashioning herself as "deserter," Clare manifests neither signs of racial self-hatred nor a deep-seated desire to be white. And while it is true that Clare ultimately expresses boredom and disillusionment with her "pale existence," her story fails to conform to the convention of the tragic mulatta who typically experiences guilt and remorse resulting from racial "desertion" or "abandonment." As Irene later describes her,

> ... it wasn't ... that Clare cared at all about the race or what was to become of it. She didn't. Or that she had for any of its members great, or even real, affection.... Nor could it be said that she had even the slightest artistic or sociological interest in the race that some members of other races dis-

played. She hadn't. No, Clare Kendry cared nothing for the race. She only belonged to it.

Thus, unlike the more conventional black portrayal of the tragic mulatta who anguishes over her desertion of the black "race," Larsen's Clare, "determined . . . to be a person and not a charity or a problem, or even a daughter of the indiscreet Ham," decides to cross the color line in order to "get all the things [she] wanted and never had had." Having gained entry into a white world of wealth and privilege through marriage to an affluent banker, Clare returns only to escape, in the excitement and gaiety she discovers in Harlem, the sterility of a staid white environment. Her "return," so to speak, seems motivated no less by her "having" nature ("Clare always had a . . . having way with her") than her previous decision to pass. In short, while implicitly calling into question a system of racial and gender privilege, Larsen's character would seem to represent what Barbara Christian calls "the not so tragic mulatta" who is neither racial repentant nor racial rebel.

Larsen's novel refuses to easily surrender its meaning to the questing reader or probing critic. And read as a (post)modernist text, it makes certain demands on the critic and reader, demands that are signaled symbolically in Larsen's revision of the conventional tragic mulatto as modern passing subject as well as formally in its critical self-reflexivity, narrative ellipses, and dramatic equivocations. The opening of the text, a personal retrospective occurring long after the events rehearsed have transpired, is signified by the opening of a letter. At the outset of Part One ("Encounter"), Irene receives a missive from Clare, a childhood friend whom she has accidently encountered while they were both socially passing in the rooftop tearoom of the fashionable, whites-only Drayton Hotel in Chicago. Here, the reader is introduced to Irene, who muses over a letter addressed in a handwriting she recognizes to be that of her mysterious friend. This "scene of reading," as it were, establishes a structural equivalence between Irene and the reader on the one hand and Clare's letter and Larsen's text on the other.

Unlike Deborah McDowell, who reads the envelope as a "metaphoric vagina," I am more inclined to agree with Claudia Tate that it functions as a kind of foreshadowing device, an Eliotian "objective correlative" of Clare's character "daring defiance of unwritten codes of social propriety."[51] Beyond the letter's metonymic significance, however, I would suggest that the *unopened* envelope—while broadly signifying the dangers of writing—functions, paradoxically, as a metaphor of concealment and *safe enclosure*. Thus the enclosed content of the envelope would figure, on one level, as the *textual unconscious*—that which is risky, unsafe, or menacing. Irene, as addressee, then, faces the challenge of opening the letter and confronting the potential dangers of the *psychic unconscious*.

The structural parallels between Irene/the reader and Clare's letter/Larsen's text provide an early narrative clue on how to read Larsen's novel. What the reader/critic subsequently recognizes is that, for Irene, Clare embodies a "performative" text, and more precisely, the performativity of what legal historian Eva Saks elsewhere describes as "the miscegenous body."[52] Clare (whose name means "light") performs "whiteness" and suppresses "blackness" in the "miscegenous body"—a body in which the "races" (*genus*) are mixed (*miscere*). The contents of Clare's letters articulate the "black" text concealed within the "white" body, expressing her despair with "this pale life" and her "longing . . . for that other. . . ." At the heart of Larsen's novel, then, is Irene's *readerly performance* juxtaposed to Clare's *textual performance*. Clare as text—as performative text— becomes a work of art and artifice ("one got . . . [an] aesthetic pleasure from watching her"), and, as such, an object of *desire* and *knowing* for Irene and the spectatorial reader. And it is here, in the realm of desire for knowledge (of Self and Other), rather than in latent lesbian desire, that I would locate Clare's true seductiveness for Irene—as well as the seductiveness of the text for the reader.[53] Like Balzac's Zambinella, Clare functions as an illusion, an actress, a sign, a performer who epitomizes not only difference, but the unrepresentability of difference when it is coded as the miscegenous body. Clare's body, figured in the body of the letter, remains an indecipherable text, an illegible sign, an object of knowledge to be "read," repressed, and, finally, repudiated by Irene. Fundamentally coded as surface and artifice, Clare is produced primarily as "affect." When, for example, Irene visits Clare at the exclusive Morgan, she discovers herself

in a sitting-room, large and high, at whose windows hung startlingly blue draperies which triumphantly dragged attention from the gloomy chocolate-colored furniture. And Clare was wearing a thin floating dress of the same shade of blue, which suited her and the rather difficult room to perfection.

Elsewhere, Clare "[sits] with an air of indifferent assurance, as if arranged for, desired." In these passages, the combination of posture, costume, set, and props, as it were, contrives to achieve a spectacularly dramatic effect in which Clare gets featured stage center.

The opening scene also alerts the reader to the importance of the materiality of the letter (and perhaps, belles lettres). Significantly, here it is not so much the signified (content) as the materiality of the signifier (form) that Irene "reads." Yet even when the contents of the letter are revealed, Irene finds herself "puzzling out, as best she could, the carelessly formed words or making instinctive guesses at them." Thus, the illegibility of the letter simultaneously underscores Clare's inscrutability, the elusiveness of the text, and Irene's readerly incompetence. Later, that same inscrutability is written into "the look on Clare's . . . face," which Irene finds "unfathomable, utterly beyond any experience or comprehension of hers." Importantly, the reader's introduction to both Irene and Clare is framed by the act of reading and being read. And just as Clare becomes the text that Irene must learn to decipher, so Irene, in turn, becomes the text to be deciphered by the reader. What defines this moment, then, is a scene of reading in which the miscegenous text, a stand-in for the miscegenous body, results in "a crisis of representation."[54] At stake in this crisis of representation is the incongruity between the visible sign and the social and legal meaning of the body. While legally defined as black, both Irene and Clare possess "unmarked bodies" in that both lack the visible markers of blackness.

This crisis of representation, moreover, is textually embodied in the form and structure of *Passing*. Through its narrative gaps and repressions, as well as its open-ended resistance to closure and resolution, Larsen's novel performs as an early exemplar of black (post)modernist indeterminacy. Thus, in spite of its modernist affinities, Larsen's narrative would seem to be best understood in terms of a contemporary (post)modernist perspective, both in the performance of its narrative strategies and structure as well as in the philosophical assumptions grounding its notions of personal and textual identity. As we shall see, the narrative retrospective is punctuated by gaps and ambiguities that ultimately function to expose the contingency of knowledge, to interrogate both racial essentialism and constructionism, and to decenter the autonomous and desiring subject.[55] The repressions of this "writerly" text leave it to the reader, finally, to "fill in" the gaps and lacunae, thereby reconstituting the miscegenous text/body.[56] What is at stake here is the readerly reconstitution of a fragmented and/or suppressed social (and textual) identity.

Since the message of the letter (text) is only partially revealed, its full meaning is, in effect, repressed. Not only do the textual ellipses and narrative gaps represent the textual unconscious, but Irene's own repressions as central consciousness leave it to the reader to fill in the textual occlusions. Mindful that the challenge in reading the text is prefigured by Irene's encounter with Clare's letter, the reader/critic, like Irene, must attempt to elicit the mystery of its meaning—to uncover the secret of the text (figured in some respects by the secrecy of Clare's passing). It is indeed only by filling in the gaps of Larsen's elusive, elliptical, and equivocal novel—a mode of reading that is demanded by the strategies of (post)-modernism—that the critic/reader is potentially able to reconstitute the meaning of the miscegenous text/body.

Again, the reader must bear in mind that Clare is represented only through Irene, thus allowing Clare only secondary characterization. Metaphorically, Clare's interiority is a gap within the text; her inner life (including her hidden identity) remains sealed in the envelope, whose contents (like Clare herself) are later destroyed by Irene. And like the envelope, which bears no return address, its sender is associated with no precise place or origins (although she travels and resides in New York, Chicago, and Europe). Clare, as we shall see, functions as a kind of textualized network of surfaces on which Irene reads (writes) her own psychic projection of otherness. Significantly, upon their first encounter, Irene is figured as a reader who "[fills] in the gap of her history," while Clare—constructed as a surface that lacks depth and interiority—is rendered "silent." But it is her aversive glance ("she had only to turn away her eyes, to refuse [Clare] recognition") that restricts Irene's knowledge of the Otherness that is Clare. For the reader, then, the meaning of Clare's character remains buried in Irene's unconscious and the textual unconscious.

Structured by three chapters, "Encounter," "Re-encounter," and "Finale," Larsen's novel structurally mimes and formally thematizes a theatrical performance. The second "act," as it were, opens with Irene ruminating over a missive she had received from Clare some two years earlier—"a letter that was, to her taste, a bit too lavish in its wordiness, a shade too unreserved in the manner of its expression." Not only is Clare further textualized in this passage, but she is associated in Irene's imagery with an aesthetics of theatricality or performativity (her face is an "ivory mask") whose affect is excess: "It roused again that old suspicion that Clare was acting, not consciously, perhaps—that is, not too consciously—but, none the less, acting." Clare's excess is expressed not only in what is elsewhere described as her "theatrical heroics," but in her dress, which "deliberate[ly] court[ed] . . . attention"; in her language, characterized by "all those superlatives"; in her smile, which is "a shade too provocative"; and in her appearance, which renders her "just a shade too good-looking." But if Clare is a duplicitously performative text, associated with *excess*, Irene is arguably an unreliable narrator, associated with *lack*. Indeed, it is Irene's psychic anxiety and repression that is reflected in the narrative's gaps and anxieties. Put somewhat differently, if Clare signals a kind of psychic exhibitionism, Irene figures a psychic repression manifest both at the level of the body (sexual repression) as well as narrative (textual repression). But although the reader may indeed share Irene's fear and fascination with the text (Clare) as an aestheticized object of knowledge, Irene's repressive reading need not be the reader/critic's.

Significantly, it is Irene who, at the outset of the novel, fears "being ejected"—or "outed," as it were—from the racially exclusive Drayton Hotel tearoom.[57] What soon becomes evident, however, is that Irene's true "outing" is a consequence of her re-encounter with Clare Kendry, whose "daring" and "having" ways expose Irene to her own alterity, or "otherness."

Arguing that Clare, in fact, exists in terms of Irene's own projections of "otherness" ("the unconscious, the unknowable, the erotic, and the passive"), Cheryl Wall figures Irene and Clare as psychological "doubles."[58] Similarly, for Thadious Davis, Clare embodies "the personal and psychological characteristics that Irene needs to become a complete person."[59] Further, Ann duCille figures Clare as "something more than . . . another doubling or dividing"; for duCille, Clare functions less as Irene's "alter ego than her alter libido, the buried, long-denied sexual self."[60] Like these readings, my own assumes a relation of complementarity between Irene and Clare, in which the latter functions to disrupt Irene's sense of identity by exposing her long-repressed self-difference.

In her portrayal of these two women as mirror-like images, Larsen frequently subverts the opposition claimed by Irene: "Actually they were strangers. Strangers in their ways and means of living. Strangers in their desires and ambitions. Strangers even in their racial consciousness." Yet Larsen's character development would suggest that although Irene poses as a proponent of race uplift who professes to be repelled by Clare's passing, she remains intrigued, and "[wishes] to find out about this hazardous business [passing]. . . ." Upon meeting Clare's husband, the racist Bellew, Irene *"conceal*[s] *her own origins."* In denying her race, Irene, in effect, "passes," thus reinforcing her identity with Clare. Further, searching for "some clue to [Clare's] identity," Irene feels that "about the woman was some quality, *an intangible something, too vague to define, too remote to seize,* but which was, to Irene Redfield, *very familiar.*" Clare possesses a "quality of feeling that was to [Irene] *strange, even repugnant*" yet somehow *"compelling"* (italics mine). Later, Irene perceives that Clare has the ability to "put into words that which, not so definitely defined, was so often in her own heart ..." At other times, Irene remarks that it was "as if she [Irene] had been in the secret of the other's [Clare's] thoughts," and that it was "uncanny, the way Clare could divine what one was thinking." Such a complex relation of psychic projection and introjection defines a relation lvi · Critical Foreword

of deep intersubjectivity between these characters, one in which Clare functions, on multiple levels, as a kind of doppleganger for Irene. Significantly, Clare addresses Irene as " 'Rene," thereby erasing the "I" in "Irene." In doing so, Clare, in effect, exposes (I)Rene to her long-buried other self, one that threatens to disrupt the placid surface of her safe and orderly life. The clear affinity between these characters is signaled metaphorically at the outset of the novel in the scene of "encounter" at the downtown Chicago hotel when Irene notes that "the woman sitting on the other side of the table [holds] for [her] a fascination, strange and compelling." In effect, this mirroring of the self ("on the other side of the table") sets the stage for Irene's ambivalent negotiation of the difference and identity between herself and a figure toward whom she feels both aversion and attraction.

Irene's ambivalence invokes the logic of a contemporary psychoanalytic discourse of identification and difference. Essential to Irene's sense of "permanence, safety, and security" is the repression of her own otherness—the alterity and *self-difference* that is embodied by Clare. This complex relation of difference and identity—and *difference in identity*—suggests that, for Larsen, the mulatto/passing subject becomes a trope not only for difference or *otherness*, but more precisely for self-difference, or the *otherness of the self*.

Larsen, in effect, externalizes the internal drama of difference and identity that is staged in her first novel, *Quicksand*. If, in her earlier novel, the protagonist Helga Crane seeks to reduce her multiplicity and self-difference to sameness (which leads to her certain death), in *Passing*, the central characters are figured as fractured and self-divided, such that each represents not only the *other of the self*, but the *otherness of the self*. In other words, in her second novel, Larsen fractures and externalizes the equivocal drama of identity that is internalized by the protagonist of her first.

—

Like Clare's letter (and Larsen's novel), "race" proves to be a subtle and elusive text, not easily read. As argued above, the passing plot would seem to fundamentally destabilize the color line; nevertheless, like other Harlem Renaissance black writers, Larsen seems, at times, to support an essentialist view of blackness, thereby affirming Samira Kawash's proposition that the narrative of passing is "necessarily constructed around the presumption of the existence of fixed and irrevocable racial identities because it is only in relation to such a conception of race that passing is possible in the first place."[61] At the outset of the novel, Irene seems to challenge a biologically constructed notion of race:

> Absurd! Impossible! White people were so stupid about such things for all that they usually asserted that they were able to tell; and by the most ridiculous means, finger-nails, palms of hands, shapes of ears, teeth, and other equally silly rot.

Yet her dismissal of the physical markers by which some purport to read racial difference seems contradicted by her later conviction that Clare possesses "Negro eyes": "Ah! Surely! They were Negro eyes! mysterious and concealing. And set in that ivory face under that bright hair, there was about them something exotic."[62] Irene's husband, Brian, also suggests that there is something peculiar and unique (and therefore essentializing) about race. Reflecting on the phenomenon of racial passing, Brian concludes that "they [passers] always come back. I've seen it happen time and time again." Answering Irene's query, "But why?," Brian replies, "If I knew that, I'd know what race is." It is for this reason that in response to Hugh Wentworth, the white novelist and friend who ponders over "the trick" of how to "pick some of 'em [the passers]," Irene explains that "[n]obody can [detect who is passing]. Not by looking." Her explanation here is significant because it suggests that racial difference lies neither in physical "appearance," nor from anything "[done] or said," but rather in "ways [that are not] definite or tangible." Clearly, for Irene, "race" or "racial difference," while discernible by the freemasonry of the race, is something that is neither palpable nor definable. If Larsen's passing plot, then, destabilizes the notion of race, her characters essentialize race, and if Clare demonstrates the construction of race through racial performativity, Irene would seem first biologically and later metaphysically to essentialize race by abstracting notions of race and race difference from history and culture.

As suggested above, the passing novel also enables the reader to examine the construction of whiteness from a racial location. If it is true, as Ruth Frankenberg argues, that one of the prerogatives of whiteness is to make "itself invisible precisely by asserting its normalcy, its transparency," then it is the African American passing novel that "marks" and "names" whiteness and white privilege.[63] These stories of passing implicitly pose the question asked by turn-of-the-century novelist Charles Chesnutt, "What Is a White Man?"—or, in white novelist George Washington Cable's subsequent elaboration, "What is a white woman?"[64] In *de-scribing* the markers of whiteness as appropriated by the passing subject as racial Other, novelists such as Larsen *in-scribe* whiteness as a system or configuration of signs to be manipulated in the assertion and performance of whiteness.

Clearly, for the author, whiteness is attached not only to social privilege but to a materialist ethic: John Bellew, Clare's white husband, "turn[s] up from South America with untold gold." Thus, not only is the flagrantly racist Bellew attached to lucre, but suggestively to the imperialistic exploitation of a land and its natural resources in the pursuit of money and wealth. And furthermore, although curiously associated with "latent physical power," Bellew is constructed as something of a male hysteric, manifested in his blatant and unrestrained racist vituperation, as well as in his enervated and effeminate demeanor (he possesses "a soft mouth, somewhat womanish, set in an unhealthy-looking dough-colored face"). Bellew's effeminacy and hysteria must also be read in terms of the racist, albeit affectionate, epithet that Bellew confers on his wife, Clare, who is, unbeknownst to her husband, of African American descent. Humorously, Bellew explains why he calls his wife "Nig": "When

we were first married, she [Clare] was as white as . . .
a lily. But I declare she's gettin' darker and darker. I
tell her if she don't look out, she'll wake up one of
these days and find she's turned into a nigger." In response to Clare's question, "My goodness, Jack! What
difference would it make if, after all these years, you
were to find out that I was one or two percent colored?," he answers, "Oh, no, Nig . . . nothing like that
with me. I know you're no nigger, so it's all right. You
can get as black as you please as far as I'm concerned,
since I know you're no nigger. I *draw the line* at that.
No niggers in my family. Never have been and never
will be" (italics mine). In order to secure his own
white masculinity, potentially destabilized by his desire for the "exotic other" figured by Clare, Bellew
must *draw the (color) line* while, at the same time, fet-
ishizing the object of his fear and desire—the "blackness" of "Nig's" body.[65]

Buried in Larsen's text is an obscure but significant
reference to the Rhinelander case, a controversial
and highly publicized court trial that can be classified
as a part of American miscegenation jurisprudence.
While Irene's seemingly offhand reference concern-
ing the Rhinelander case dramatizes the potential
legal consequences of Clare's "transgression," it also
demonstrates the power of legal discourse to define,

construct, and even to criminalize the miscegenous body. Further, it is a case that emphasizes the discrepancy between the visible markers and the legal definition of race that leads to a "crisis of representation" in the social construction of the miscegenous body. Linking Bellew's comments to Irene's reference to the notorious Rhinelander case highlights the function of the "line" that Bellew "draws" and its demarcation in the courts by means of miscegenation laws designed to protect white property rights as well as the rights of whiteness. Unknowingly, however, Bellew has formed a conjugal alliance that consequently reproduces the miscegenous body within his own family, an action that unwittingly gives the lie to his own claims of racial purity.

Thus, it is the "dangerous mixing" of "white blood" and "black blood" that constitutes a threat not only to white property inheritance, but to the "purity of the white body politic." The passing body, in particular, is a site of danger since, by betraying no racialized markers, it renders blackness invisible. Not only does Bellew's racist invective express the fears and anxieties of white masculinity around issues of race, race difference, and miscegenation, but Irene's reference to the Rhinelander case calls attention to collective white race anxieties and fears as reflected in American jurisprudence. Basically this case represents for white society an expression of the anxiety over race-mixing, both in its potential to change distribution of property (which is precisely what happened in the Rhinelander case),[66] as well as in its threat to pollute the putative racial purity of the white family, race, and nation.

The issues of race and nation are also raised, albeit somewhat obliquely, in the affinity between Brian and Clare. Irene apparently (mis)reads the relationship between her husband and her friend as one of betrayal and infidelity, and characteristically, the text refuses to affirm or undermine Irene's perceptions, leaving it to the reader/critic to reach his or her own conclusions. However, I would propose a reading that would both affirm and challenge Irene's suspicions. Like Clare, Brian is a figure animated by a desire for a life outside the racist proscriptions of American society. His brooding discontent and innate dissatisfaction stem from his "dislike and disgust for his profession and his country." And curiously, like John Bellew, Brian is attracted to South America. Irene has "[made] . . . strenuous efforts to repress . . . that old, queer, unhappy restlessness . . . that craving for some place strange and different . . ." that often leads to Brian's moodiness. Arguably, what Irene suspects to

be a sexual attraction between Clare and Brian reflects an affinity of desire for social and personal freedom from the confines of race in the United States.
Brian's response to American racial arrangements,
like Clare's, constitutes an option (escape) that, like
passing, is available only to individuals. What identifies these characters symbolically, then, is that both
seek to cross the line, Brian geographically and Clare
racially. Brian's desire to cross geographical borders
("rush off to that remote place of his heart's desire")
functions, in effect, as the symbolic equivalent of
Clare's desire to cross racial boundaries in pursuit of
wealth and status. The symbolic equivalence between
expatriation and passing suggests here what Samira
Kawash calls "geographies of the color line," that is to
say, the metaphorical relation between race and geography in which, as David Goldberg explains, "spatial
distinctions . . . are racialized [and] racial categories [are] spatialized."[67] In addition, Larsen's symbolic equivalence of race and geography fractures
the choices that James Weldon Johnson's narrator col-
lapses in his rationale for passing in *The Autobiography
of an Ex-Colored Man:* "I argued to forsake one's race to
better one's condition was no less worthy an action
than to forsake one's country for the same purpose."[68]
Thus, Larsen's intertextual response to Johnson fig-

ures both Clare and potentially Brian (like the ex-colored man) as "racial expatriates" who transgress the geography of the color line. In fact, Irene's description of passing—"the breaking away from all that was familiar and friendly to take one's chance in another environment"—implicates race and place in a definition that could serve equally well for "expatriation." But, of course, as a racially marked body, Brian "couldn't exactly pass." (Unlike Clare, however, whose blackness is invisible, Brian's complexion is "of an exquisitely fine texture and deep copper color.")

If Brian and Clare each repudiates boundaries of race and nationality, Irene, on the other hand, seeks to repress Brian's expatriate impulse and to deny Clare's passing preference. For Irene, expatriation, like passing, represents "a dangerous business," that is to say, a threat to her own desires for "safety," "security," and "permanence" in her own life. Not only does Irene avow her ties to race, but also her ties to nation: ". . . she would not go to Brazil. She belonged in this land of rising towers. She was an American. She grew from this soil, and she would not be uprooted." Here Larsen affirms for her protagonist a complex sense of self-definition predicated not only upon racial identity, but an affirmation of national identity and identification.

———

Although Larsen revises the conventional treatment of the tragic mulatta, the death of Clare in the "Finale" would seem to replicate the formulaic conclusion of the nineteenth-century passing narrative. Typically, the earlier novel of passing ended with the death of the passer who is caught, unhappily, betwixt and between the black and white worlds. Insofar as Clare has no place in the social order and, therefore, must exit the text, Larsen would seem to conform to conventions of the tragic mulatta. In the more traditional treatment of the passing novel, the existing racial order is restored and the essentialist assumptions underpinning that order are affirmed. Clare's successful performance of whiteness, however, effectively disrupts the social order and reduces essentialism to a virtual absurdity. Nevertheless, Clare's performance comes at a high price indeed— her death.

Most critics and readers agree that the reasons for Clare's death remain inconclusive. Either she falls, jumps, or is pushed from a sixth-story window, thus rendering her death either an accident, suicide, or homicide. And there is, as Claudia Tate warns, "no tangible proof to support one interpretation over another."[69] Nonetheless, the inevitability of Clare's death is signaled throughout the text by images that foreshadow Clare's fate: the "offending letter," which Irene "[tears] into tiny ragged squares" and scatters over the train's railing, and, later, Irene's "boiling rage" resulting in a "slight crash" and a "shattered cup," leaving "dark stains [which] dotted the bright rug." Indeed, her death is unwittingly anticipated by Brian as he, Clare, and Irene climb up to the sixth-story apartment of the Freelands to attend a Christmas party; Brian jokingly tells Clare, "Mind . . . you don't fall by the wayside . . ." Moments later, Clare's death is again prefigured by Irene who, opening the "long casement-windows of which the Freelands were so proud," then "finished her cigarette and threw it out, watching the tiny spark drop slowly down to the white ground below."

In the conclusion of the novel, Irene hears "a strange man" attributing the event to "death by misadventure," and while it seems likely that Clare's death, on the surface of it, could be the consequence of an accident or mishap, it is equally true that both Bellew and Irene must be regarded as co-implicated in her demise. Earlier Irene desperately desires Clare's death, becoming "faint and sick" while trying vainly to "drive away" the thought that "[i]f Clare should die," she could rid herself of the "menace" to permanence that Clare represents for her. And arguably, it is Irene's aphasia, or "[failure] to speak," about her inadvertent encounter with Bellew that leads ultimately to Clare's death. On the verge of telling Clare about the meeting with Bellew, Irene fears that "Clare wouldn't avert the results of the encounter [exposure of her racial identity]," and represses "the flood of speech on her lips." In some respects, then, Clare's death can surely be construed as the indirect consequence of Irene's "keeping back information." However, if Irene's aphasia leads indirectly to Clare's discovery, it is Bellew's verbal accusation—"So you're a nigger, a damned dirty nigger!"—that, as we have seen, redraws the color line. In so doing, Bellew verbally "pushes" Clare across that line—over which she stumbles. Bellew's speech is, in its affect, performative: The moment of its utterance coincides with the moment of Clare's fatal fall to her death, symbolically through the blackness of night into the whiteness of the snow below.

Yet however one reads Clare's death, the reader must inevitably return to Irene who, through an act of memory ("Such were Irene Redfield's memories"), produces a narrative that is fundamentally, albeit fragmentarily, reconstituted through the various scenes of reading that structure her narrative. At the novel's conclusion, Irene is rendered incapable of reliably reading or remedying her own situation; her story achieves neither resolution nor closure. Rather than invoke her narrative as a modernist stay against chaos, Irene sinks into virtual unconsciousness:

> [Irene's] quaking knees gave way under her. She moaned and sank down, moaned again. Through the great heaviness that submerged and drowned her she was dimly conscious. . . . *Then everything was dark*. [Italics mine.]

Significantly, Irene's subsequent memory lapse replicates the textual equivocations and ellipses that are typical of (post)modernist narrative:

> What happened next, Irene Redfield never afterwards allowed herself to remember. Never clearly. . . .
> What would the others think? That Clare had fallen? That she had deliberately leaned backward? Certainly one or the other. Not— . . .
> She stammered: "Is she—is she—?" . . .
> . . . She just fell, before anybody could stop her. I—

In an attempt to maintain the modernist ideals of order and harmony in her world, Irene has attempted to discipline and regulate her life, as well as that of her husband and sons, for "Irene didn't like change, particularly changes that affected her smooth routine of her household." Just as Irene represses her husband's desire for Brazil, so she represses, much to Brian's dismay and protest, the discussion of certain subjects in her household in an attempt to protect her sons from the knowledge of ideas such as "sex" and the "race problem." Thus Irene attempts to repress not only self-knowledge, but the knowledge of others that she construes to be threatening or dangerous (and significantly that "knowledge" is "racial" and "sexual" knowledge). Yet Irene cannot escape "that fear which crouched, always deep down within her, stealing away that sense of security, the feeling of permanence, from the life which she so admirably arranged for them all, and desired so ardently to remain as it was." But as Irene's final physical collapse suggests, it is she herself who embodies internally the disorder and instability that seem to menace the surface order and organization of her world. In a moment of epiphany, Irene recognizes that although "life went on precisely as before . . . she . . . had changed." It is "knowing" that "had changed her": Invoking the image of the Platonic cave, Irene reflects, "It was as if in a house long dim, a match had been struck, showing ghastly shapes where had been only blurred shadows." Irene's illuminations, however, are submerged in the conclusion by a memory lapse and a final fall into unconsciousness. Irene must "black out" her epiphany, as well as its catalyst and agent, Clare.

Metaphorically, then, it is the opening of the envelope, the door into a repressed or buried consciousness, that exposes Irene to the repressed knowledge of self-difference and that results ironically in tragedy for Clare. For, finally, the death of Clare represents Irene's successful repression of self-difference. Symbolically, Irene's "hand on Clare's arm" links them corporeally in that final equivocal moment. If Clare indeed represents aspects of the self that Irene seeks to deny, then Clare's death—whether accident, homicide, or suicide—represents the death of Irene's "otherness." In other words, the "other" in Irene effectively commits suicide. Put differently, Clare's physical death functions as the equivalent of Irene's psychic suicide.

Although the *cause* of Clare's death remains indeterminate, what is of greater importance is the *fact* of her death, and its necessity at the level of modernist narrative. Clare's transgressive performance of whiteness is "punished," as it were, by the elaborate essentialist conceptions of her husand and Irene. Narratively, Irene's nationalist essentialism combines with Bellew's racialist essentialism to, in effect, reinforce the color line by "killing off" Clare. As author, Larsen's dilemma is that she has created a character who, through the successful performance of whiteness, demonstrates the falsity of black nationalist essentialism on the one hand and white racial essentialism on the other. However, Larsen's successful refutation is not without a cost for both author and character, a cost prefigured in terms of a kind of discourse of the debt that threads through the novel. Importantly, at the outset of the novel, Clare informs her friend, "In fact, all things considered, I think, 'Rene, that [passing is] even worth the price." Later, quoting her father, Clare expresses a similar sentiment: "As my inestimable dad used to say, 'Everything must be paid for,' " a phrase later eerily repeated by Irene.

The author, in other words, incurs a debt that her character must "pay" with the sacrifice of her life. (Surely it is ironically significant that Clare's death, which occurs on Christmas, is meant to suggest something of a sacrifice to the dominant notions of essentialized racial identity.) Clare has, in effect, *lived out* the complex identity that Larsen's narrative has *theorized*. At the level of character and narrative, the essentialist divide is finally revealed to be illusory. And Clare's exposure, in full view of Irene and Bellew, ensures her own disappearance in a world of modernity saturated by an essentialist conception of race. Clearly, at this point Clare is left with no place to occupy in the racially essentialized world of modernity: Irene will not allow her to assume an identity in the black world; Bellew will not allow her to assume an identity in the white world. Yet Clare goes on to claim a postmodernist identity that is predicated on self-difference and an identity that challenges Irene's modernist self-sameness. Clare performs, and lives out, an identity that is foreign to Irene's modernist conception of integral identity. In fact, Clare's complexly reconstructed identity is fundamentally inconsistent and incompatible with the essentializing assumptions of her culture. Larsen has created a character, a mulatta, who affirms a complex, contingent, and multiplicitous postmodernist notion of identity in a modernist world that would nullify her very existence. Her continued existence would menace both Bellew's and Irene's world, so she must cease to exist.

Clare's successful passing from one "essence"

("blackness") to another diametrically opposed "essence" ("whiteness") demonstrates, finally, that these so-called essences are not biological but socially constructed. Larsen's artistic achievement lies in the narrative performance of her refutation of essentialism. She does not challenge the presuppositions of essentialism either morally, philosophically, or scientifically; rather through the performativity of her narrative, she presents a reductio ad absurdum refutation of the essentialist position. As author, Larsen imagines a position that her narrative demonstrates to entail an absurdity. In other words, the presumption of essentialism would make it impossible for one to switch "essences." It is precisely the successful performance of passing that would render such a presumption absurd.

Just as Irene, in the final scene, sinks into unconsciousness and later, a memory gap, Clare falls into a kind of metaphysical gap. Clare's fall into a metaphysical hole has its counterpart in both the textual "holes" as well as the "holes" in Irene's memory. Such a conclusion can only confirm that there exists no place in the realm of essentialist being for Clare's continued existence; she possesses no ontological claim in the world of essentialized modernity.

Notes

1. See James de Jongh's *Vicious Modernism* (Cambridge, Mass.: Cambridge University Press, 1990).

2. Werner Sollors, *Neither Black Nor White Yet Both* (New York: Oxford University Press, 1997), 247–48.

3. Rita Felski, *The Gender of Modernity* (Cambridge, Mass.: Harvard University Press, 1995), 13.

4. Arthur Davis, for instance, speculates that "the present-day reader may wonder at this morbid concern . . . with the passing theme" (*From the Dark Tower: Afro-American Writers, 1900–1960* [Washington, D.C.: Howard University Press, 1974], 6). This sentiment is shared by Amritjit Singh, Hoyt Fuller, and other earlier critics of the genre.

5. W.E.B. Du Bois, *The Crisis* (1929); also cited in Hoyt Fuller's Introduction, Nella Larsen, *Passing* (New York: Collier Books, 1971), 13.

6. According to Gayle Wald, the "postpassing" narratives "[articulate] collective values of pride in the 'Negro' identity and [challenge] the social and economic pressures that promote passing as an 'alternative' to racial segregation." Gayle Wald, *Crossing the Color Line: Racial Passing in Twentieth-Century U.S. Literature and Culture* (Durham: Duke University Press, 2000), 119.

7. See Claudia Tate, "Nella Larsen's *Passing:* A Problem of Interpretation," *Black American Literary Forum* (Winter 1980), 146.

8. W.E.B. Du Bois, *The Crisis* (1928); also cited in Hiroko Sato, "Under the Harlem Shadow: A Study of Jessie Fauset and Nella Larsen," in *Harlem Renaissance Remembered: Essays,* Arna Bontemps, ed. (New York: Dodd, Mead, & Co., 1972).

9. W.E.B. Du Bois, *The Crisis* (July 1929), 234; also cited in Fuller.

10. Robert Bone, *The Negro Novel in America* (New Haven: Yale University Press, 1958; revised 1965), 102.

11. Fuller, 18.

12. Sato, 88, 89.

13. Nathan Irvin Huggins, *Harlem Renaissance* (New York: Oxford University Press, 1971), 157, 159.

14. David Levering Lewis, *When Harlem Was in Vogue* (New York: Knopf, 1981; Oxford University Press, 1989), 231.

15. George Hutchinson, "Subject to Disappearance: Interracial Identity in Nella Larsen's *Quicksand*," in Genevieve Fabre and Michel Feith, *Temples for Tomorrow: Looking Back at the Harlem Renaissance* (New York: Oxford University Press, 2001).

16. Cheryl A. Wall, *Women of the Harlem Renaissance* (Bloomington and Indianapolis: Indiana University Press, 1995), 132.

17. See Charles R. Larson, *Invisible Darkness: Jean Toomer & Nella Larsen* (Iowa City: University of Iowa Press, 1993), 86, and Thadious M. Davis, *Nella Larsen, Novelist of the Harlem Renaissance: A Woman's Life Unveiled* (Baton Rouge: Louisiana State University Press, 1994). Arthur Davis describes Larsen's first novel as "a moving story," although "not as good a novel as *Quicksand*," 97. Critic Bernard Bell regards *Quicksand* as "structurally ... the better of [Larsen's] two novels" (*The Afro-American Novel and Its Tradition* [Amherst: The University of Massachusetts Press, 1987], 110). And although questioning the grounds of earlier evaluations of *Passing*, Mary Mabel Youman does not "quarrel with the overall [critical] judgment" that ranks Larsen's second novel "inferior" to her first.

18. Gayle Wald aptly deploys this term.

19. This is the second version of William Wells Brown's *Clotel, or, the President's Daughter* (1853), which is currently regarded as the first novel published by an African American.

20. See David Kirkpatrick's account, "On Long-Lost Pages, a Female Slave's Voice" (*The New York Times,* Nov. 11, 2001), which provides the account of Henry Louis Gates Jr.'s remarkable "discovery" of this volume.

21. Werner Sollors speculates that "[t]he first American instances in which the word 'passing' was used to signify 'crossing the color line' would seem to have appeared in notices concern-

ing runaway slaves, and the term 'passing'—first for 'free,' and then for (its larger part-synonym) 'white'—may have entered American fiction through the citing of such bills," 255.

22. Caleb Johnson, "Crossing the Color Line," *Outlook and Independent* 158 (Aug. 26, 1931): 526; also cited in Sollors, 245.

23. Walter White, "Why I Remain a Negro," *The Saturday Review of Literature,* Oct. 22, 1947; quoted in Amritjit Singh, *The Novels of the Harlem Renaissance: Twelve Black Writers, 1923–1933* (University Park: The Pennsylvania State University Press), 92.

24. Gunnar Myrdal, *An American Dilemma: The Negro Problem and Modern Democracy* (New York and London: Harper & Brothers, 1944), 683, 688.

25. Sterling Brown, *The Negro in American Fiction* (1937; reprint, New York: Atheneum, 1969), 142.

26. See José Esteban Muñoz, *Disidentification: Queers of Color and the Performance of Politics* (Minneapolis: University of Minnesota Press, 1999).

27. Barbara Christian, *Black Women Novelists: The Development of a Tradition, 1892–1976* (Westport, Conn.: Greenwood Press, 1980), 44, 45.

28. Bone, 98.

29. Singh, 93.

30. Donald Goellnicht, "Passing as Autobiography: James Weldon Johnson's *The Autobiography of an Ex-Colored Man,*" *African-American Review* 30.1 (1996), 19.

31. Examples of works by such southern writers include Thomas Dixon's *The Clansmen* (1905) and *The Leopard's Spots* (1902), and Thomas Nelson Page's *Red Rock: A Chronicle of Reconstruction* (1898).

32. David Roediger, *The Wages of Whiteness: Race and the Making of the American Working Class* (New York: Verso, 1991); also cited in Ruth Frankenberg, *Displacing Whiteness: Essays in Social and Cultural Criticism* (Durham: Duke University Press, 1997), 10.

33. Sollors, 260.

34. Cheryl I. Harris, "Whiteness as Property," in *Critical Race The-*

ory: The Key Writings That Formed the Movement, Kimberle Cren-
shaw, Neil Gotanda, Gary Peller, and Kendall Thomas, eds.
(New York: The New Press, 1996), 278.

35. Ibid.

36. Eva Saks, "Representing Miscegenation Law," *Raritan* 8.2
(1988), 57.

37. Joel Williamson, *New People: Miscegenation and Mulattoes in the
United States* (New York: Free Press, 1980), 98.

38. Sir Francis Galton, the inventor of fingerprinting techniques,
began his project in an attempt to discover an indicator of
"Race and Temperament" in the character and patterns of fin-
gerprints. Josiah C. Nott, in his *Two Lectures on the Natural History of the Caucasian and Negro Races* (1844), moved from the
scriptural evocation of the curse of Ham to a biological argument for racial difference that was based on a theory of polygenesis. Harvard professor Louis Agassiz, who developed his
racial ideas in 1863, is widely acknowledged as one of the
major formulators of "scientistic racism." See Sollors, 157, 109,
131.

39. Drawing out the implications of British philosopher J. L.
Austin's work on performative utterances, contemporary theorists such as Jacques Derrida and Judith Butler postulate the
performativity of identities constructed through practices of
citationality and iterability. "Performativity," Judith Butler argues, "consists in a reiteration of norms which precede, con-
strain, and exceed the performer and in that sense cannot be
taken as the fabrication of the performer's 'will' or 'choice.'"
For Butler, then, "The reduction of performativity to performance would be a mistake." (Judith Butler, *Bodies That Matter*
[New York: Routledge, 1993], 234).

40. See Mary Helen Washington, "Lost Women: Nella Larsen:
Mystery Woman of the Harlem Renaissance," *Ms.* (Dec. 1980).
Arguably, of course, the same indictment could be brought
against what might be regarded as "compulsory blackness," in
which, by virtue of the one-drop rule, one's "roots and genealogy" are also denied.

41. For Wall, these roles are defined as "the perfect lady" and "the

exotic Other." Wall argues, correctly, that Irene is "the perfect lady" and Clare "the exotic Other"—both roles rejected by Larsen's earlier protagonist, Helga Crane, in *Quicksand*. See Wall, 121.

42. Deborah McDowell, Introduction, Nella Larsen, *Quicksand and Passing* (New Brunswick, N.J.: Rutgers University Press, 1986), xxx.

43. See Washington.

44. Tate, 143.

45. Wall, 138.

46. Mary V. Dearborn, *Pocahontas's Daughters: Gender and Ethnicity in American Culture* (New York: Oxford University Press, 1986), 59.

47. McDowell, xxvi, xxx. In *Bodies That Matter,* theorist Judith Butler both extends and revises McDowell's reading of *Passing* by arguing that race and sexuality are "inextricably linked, such that the text offers a way to read the racialization of [sex and] sexual conflict, 272.

48. Larson, 82.

49. See Ann duCille, *The Coupling Convention: Sex, Text, and Tradition in Black Women's Fiction* (New York: Oxford University Press, 1993), and Jennifer DeVere Brody, "Clare Kendry's 'True' Colors: Race and Class Conflict in Nella Larsen's *Passing*," *Callaloo* 15.4 (1992).

50. Critic Hazel Carby suggests that the mulatta "is a narrative device of mediation; it allows for a fictional exploration of the relationship between the races while being at the same time an imaginary expression of the relation between the races." See Hazel V. Carby, *Reconstructing Womanhood: The Emergence of the Afro-American Woman Novelist* (New York: Oxford University Press, 1987), 171. Similarly, Ann duCille describes the mulatta as "both a rhetorical device and a political strategy," 7.

51. McDowell, xxvi; Tate, 144.

52. Saks, 44.

53. See Deborah McDowell's argument, cited above, that Irene's attraction to Clare is based on latent or repressed lesbian desire.

54. Saks argues that because "the deviance of social form from legal form makes social form an unreliable sign of legal form (and vice versa), this deviance causes a crisis of representation," 63.

55. Referencing the black postmodernist subject, W. Lawrence Hogue compares the decentered subject of postmodernism to the modernist subject: "Unlike the alienated, modern subject who seeks temporal unification of the past and the future with the present, the postmodern subject is free from all metaphysical narratives, free to simply desire and want. He or she no longer seeks social change; he or she exists only to satisfy his or her own desires." See W. Lawrence Hogue, *Race, Modernity, Postmodernity: A Look at the Literatures of People of Color Since the 1960s* (Albany: State University of New York Press, 1996), 152.

56. In his *S/Z*, Roland Barthes distinguishes between *le scriptible* (the writerly) and *le lisible* (the readerly) text, the latter allowing the reader to collaborate in the production of meaning. See Roland Barthes, *S/Z*, Richard Miller, trans. (New York: Hill and Wang, 1974). Also see Wolfgang Iser's reader-response model of reading in which the "act of reading" generates new meanings, and even new identities, on the part of the reader: Wolfgang Iser, *The Implied Reader: Patterns of Communication in Prose Fiction from Bunyan to Beckett* (Baltimore: Johns Hopkins University Press, 1978) and *The Act of Reading: A Theory of Aesthetic Reception* (Baltimore: Johns Hopkins University Press, 1978). Both models of reading would seem especially useful for understanding the consequences of Irene's "act of reading" Clare.

57. My reading here signifies on Deborah McDowell's reading of Larsen's *Passing*.

58. Wall, 130. Curiously, Wall focuses on *Irene's* function as *Clare's* double, rather than vice versa. While acknowledging the mutuality of this relation of doubles, my own analysis emphasizes *Clare's role as Irene's double*.

59. Davis, *Nella Larsen: Novelist of the Harlem Renaissance*, 315.

60. duCille, 105. DuCille both challenges and expands Wall's and McDowell's readings of Irene.

61. Samira Kawash, *Dislocating the Color Line: Identity, Hybridity, and Singularity in African American Narrative* (Stanford: Stanford University Press, 1997), 18.

62. Significantly, both William Wells Brown's *Clotel* and Frank Webb's *The Garies and Their Friends* refer to the "mezzotinto" of the iris as a physical marker betraying African ancestry in the passing subject.

63. Frankenberg, 6.

64. In response to Chesnutt's article ("What Is a White Man?," New York *Independent,* May 30, 1889), Cable wrote the following: "You know that all my earlier stories about quadroons really ask this question, 'What is a white man, What is a white woman?'" George Washington Cable, letter to Charles Chesnutt, June 12, 1889. Charles Waddell Chesnutt Collection, Fisk University, Nashville; also cited in Stephen P. Knadler, "Untragic Mulatto: Charles Chesnutt and the Discourse of Whiteness," *American Literary History,* 8.3 (Fall 1966), 426–48.

65. In its draft stage, Larsen's *Passing* was entitled "Nig"—perhaps, as Thadious Davis speculates, as a "play" upon Carl Van Vechten's *Nigger Heaven* (1926). What is equally intriguing for me is that its initial title ironically echoed the then "undiscovered" novel by Harriet Wilson, entitled *Our Nig* (1859).

66. See Mark J. Madigan, "Miscegenation and 'The Dicta of Race and Class': The Rhinelander Case and Nella Larsen's *Passing,*" *Modern Fiction Studies* 36.4 (Winter 1990), and James L. Wacks, "Reading Race, Rhetoric and the Female Body: The Rhinelander Case and 1920s American Culture," senior thesis, Harvard University, 1995.

67. David Theo Goldberg, *Racist Culture, Philosophy and the Politics of Meaning* (Cambridge, Mass.: Blackwell, 1955), 185; also cited in Kawash, 8–9.

68. James Weldon Johnson, *The Autobiography of an Ex-Colored Man* (New York: Hill and Wang, 1960), 190.

69. Tate, 145.

Selected Bibliography

Berzon, Judith R. *Neither White Nor Black: The Mulatto Character in American Fiction.* New York: New York University Press, 1978.

Brody, Jennifer DeVere. "Clare Kendry's 'True' Colors: Race and Class Conflict in Nella Larsen's *Passing.*" *Callaloo* 15.4 (1992).

Bullock, Penelope. "The Mulatto in American Fiction." *Phylon* 6 (First Quarter 1945).

Butler, Judith. *Bodies That Matter: On the Discursive Limits of "Sex."* New York: Routledge, 1993.

————. "Passing, Queering: Nella Larsen's Psychoanalytic Challenge." In *Female Subjects in Black and White,* edited by Elizabeth Abel, Barbara Christian, and Helene Moglen. Berkeley: University of California Press, 1997.

Carby, Hazel V. *Reconstructing Womanhood: The Emergence of the Afro-American Woman Novelist.* New York: Oxford University Press, 1987.

Christian, Barbara. *Black Feminist Criticism: Perspectives on Black Women Writers.* New York: Pergamon Press, 1985.

————. *Black Women Novelists: The Development of a Tradition, 1892–1976.* Westport, Conn.: Greenwood Press, 1980.

Davis, Thadious M. *Nella Larsen: Novelist of the Harlem Renaissance: A Woman's Life Unveiled.* Baton Rouge: Louisiana State University Press, 1994.

————. "Nella Larsen's Harlem Aesthetic." In *The Harlem Renaissance: Revaluations,* edited by Amiritjit Singh, William Shiver, and Stanley Brodwin. New York: Garland, 1989.

————. Introduction to *Passing.* New York: Penguin, 1997.

Dearborn, Mary V. *Pocahontas's Daughters: Gender aned Ethnicity in American Culture.* New York: Oxford University Press, 1986.

duCille, Ann. *The Coupling Convention: Sex, Text, and Tradition in Black Women's Fiction.* New York: Oxford University Press, 1993.

Fabi, M. Giulia. *Passing and the Rise of the African American Novel.* Urbana and Chicago: University of Illinois Press, 2001.

Ginsberg, Elaine, ed. *Passing and the Fictions of Identity.* Durham: Duke University Press, 1996.

Horton, Merrill. "Blackness, Betrayal, and Childhood: Race and Identity in Nella Larsen's *Passing.*" *College Language Association Journal* 28:1 (Sept. 1994).

Hutchinson, George. "Subject to Disappearance: Interracial Identity in Nella Larsen's *Quicksand.*" In Genevieve Fabre and Michel Feith, *Temples for Tomorrow: Looking Back at the Harlem Renaissance.* New York: Oxford University Press, 2001.

Kawash, Samira. *Dislocating the Color Line: Identity, Hybridity, and Singularity in African American Narrative.* Stanford: Stanford University Press, 1997.

Larsen, Nella. "The Author's Explanation." *Forum,* April 1930.

———. "Correspondence." *Opportunity,* Sept. 1926.

———. "Danish Fun." *The Brownie's Book,* July 1920.

——— [Allen Semi]. "Freedom." *Young's Magazine,* April 1926.

———. *Passing.* New York: Knopf, 1929.

———. *Quicksand.* New York: Knopf, 1928.

———. "Sanctuary." *Forum,* Jan. 1926.

———. "Three Scandinavian Games." *The Brownie's Book,* June 1920.

——— [Allen Semi]. "The Wrong Man." *Young's Magazine,* Jan. 1926.

Larson, Charles R. *Invisible Darkness: Jean Toomer & Nella Larsen.* Iowa City: University of Iowa Press, 1993.

Madigan, Mark J. "Miscegenation and 'The Dicta of Race and Class': The Rhinelander Case and Nella Larsen's *Passing.*" *Modern Fiction Studies* 36.4 (Winter 1990).

———. " 'Then everything was dark'? The Two Endings of Nella Larsen's *Passing.*" *Papers of the Bibliographical Society of America,* 84:4 (Dec. 1990).

McDowell, Deborah, ed. Introduction to *Passing and Quicksand.* New Brunswick, N.J.: Rutgers University Press, 1986.

McLendon, Jacquelyn Y. *The Politics of Color in the Fiction of Jessie Fauset and Nella Larsen.* Charlottesville: University Press of Virginia, 1995.

————. "Self-Representation as Art in the Novels of Nella Larsen." In *Redefining Autobiography in Twentieth-Century Women's Fiction: An Essay Collection,* edited by Janice Morgan, Colette Hall, and Carol Snyder. New York: Garland Publishing, 1991.

Ramsey, Priscilla. "Freeze the Day: A Feminist Reading of Nella Larsen's *Quicksand* and *Passing.*" *Afro-American in New York Life and History* 9:1 (Jan. 1985).

Sato, Hiroko. "Under the Harlem Shadow: A Study of Jessie Fauset and Nella Larsen." In *Harlem Renaissance Remembered: Essays,* edited by Arna Bontemps. New York: Dodd, Mead, & Co., 1972.

Sollors, Werner. *Neither Black Nor White Yet Both: Thematic Explorations of Interracial Literature.* New York: Oxford University Press, 1997.

Tate, Claudia. "Nella Larsen's *Passing:* A Problem of Interpretation." *Black American Literary Forum,* Winter 1980.

Wacks, James L. "Reading Race, Rhetoric and the Female Body: The Rhinelander Case and 1920s American Culture." Senior thesis, Harvard University, 1995.

Wald, Gayle. *Crossing the Color Line: Racial Passing in Twentieth-Century U.S. Literature and Culture.* Durham: Duke University Press, 2000.

Wall, Cheryl A. "Passing for What? Aspects of Identity in Nella Larsen's Novels." *Black American Literature Forum* 20:1–2 (1980).

————. *Women of the Harlem Renaissance.* Bloomington and Indianapolis: Indiana University Press, 1995.

Washington, Mary Helen. "Lost Women: Nella Larsen: Mystery Woman of the Harlem Renaissance." *Ms.,* Dec. 1980.

Youman, Mary Mabel. "Nella Larsen's *Passing:* A Study in Irony." *College Language Association Journal* 18 (Dec. 1974).

MAE G. HENDERSON is professor of English at the University of North Carolina at Chapel Hill. Author of numerous articles on African American and feminist criticism and theory, pedagogy, and cultural studies, she is also editor of *Borders, Boundaries, and Frames;* co-editor (with John Blassingame) of the five-volume *Antislavery Newspapers and Periodicals: An Annotated Index of Letters, 1817–1871.*

FOR

Carl Van Vechten

AND

Fania Marinoff[1]

One three centuries removed
From the scenes his fathers loved,
Spicy grove, cinnamon tree,
What is Africa to me?[1]

—COUNTEE CULLEN

PART ONE

ENCOUNTER

ONE

It was the last letter in Irene Redfield's little pile of morning mail. After her other ordinary and clearly directed letters the long envelope of thin Italian paper with its almost illegible scrawl seemed out of place and alien. And there was, too, something mysterious and slightly furtive about it. A thin sly thing which bore no return address to betray the sender. Not that she hadn't immediately known who its sender was. Some two years ago she had one very like it in outward appearance. Furtive, but yet in some peculiar, determined way a little flaunting. Purple ink. Foreign paper of extraordinary size.

It had been, Irene noted, postmarked in New York

the day before. Her brows came together in a tiny frown. The frown, however, was more from perplexity than from annoyance; though there was in her thoughts an element of both. She was wholly unable to comprehend such an attitude towards danger as she was sure the letter's contents would reveal; and she disliked the idea of opening and reading it.

This, she reflected, was of a piece with all that she knew of Clare Kendry. Stepping always on the edge of danger. Always aware, but not drawing back or turning aside. Certainly not because of any alarms or feeling of outrage on the part of others.

And for a swift moment Irene Redfield seemed to see a pale small girl sitting on a ragged blue sofa, sewing pieces of bright red cloth together, while her drunken father, a tall, powerfully built man, raged threateningly up and down the shabby room, bellowing curses and making spasmodic lunges at her which were not the less frightening because they were, for the most part, ineffectual. Sometimes he did manage to reach her. But only the fact that the child had edged herself and her poor sewing over to the farthermost corner of the sofa suggested that she was in any way perturbed by this menace to herself and her work.

Clare had known well enough that it was unsafe to take a portion of the dollar that was her weekly wage for the doing of many errands for the dressmaker who lived on the top floor of the building of which Bob Kendry was janitor. But that knowledge had not deterred her. She wanted to go to her Sunday school's picnic, and she had made up her mind to wear a new dress. So, in spite of certain unpleasantness and possible danger, she had taken the money to buy the material for that pathetic little red frock.

There had been, even in those days, nothing sacrificial in Clare Kendry's idea of life, no allegiance beyond her own immediate desire. She was selfish, and cold, and hard. And yet she had, too, a strange capacity of transforming warmth and passion, verging sometimes almost on theatrical heroics.

Irene, who was a year or more older than Clare, remembered the day that Bob Kendry had been brought home dead, killed in a silly saloon-fight. Clare, who was at that time a scant fifteen years old, had just stood there with her lips pressed together, her thin arms folded across her narrow chest, staring down at the familiar pasty-white face of her parent with a sort of disdain in her slanting black eyes. For a very long time she had stood like that, silent and staring. Then, quite suddenly, she had given way to a torrent of weeping, swaying her thin body, tearing at her bright hair, and stamping her small feet. The outburst had ceased as suddenly as it had begun. She glanced quickly about the bare room, taking everyone in, even the two policemen, in a sharp look of flashing scorn. And, in the next instant, she had turned and vanished through the door.

Seen across the long stretch of years, the thing had more the appearance of an outpouring of pent-up fury than of an overflow of grief for her dead father; though she had been, Irene admitted, fond enough of him in her own rather catlike way.

Catlike. Certainly that was the word which best described Clare Kendry, if any single word could describe her. Sometimes she was hard and apparently without feeling at all; sometimes she was affectionate and rashly impulsive. And there was about her an amazing soft malice, hidden well away until provoked. Then she was capable of scratching, and very effectively too. Or, driven to anger, she would fight with a ferocity and impetuousness that disregarded or forgot any danger; superior strength, numbers, or other unfavorable circumstances. How savagely she had clawed those boys the day they had hooted her parent and sung a derisive rhyme, of their own composing, which pointed out certain eccentricities in his careening gait! And how deliberately she had—

Irene brought her thoughts back to the present, to the letter from Clare Kendry that she still held unopened in her hand. With a little feeling of apprehension, she very slowly cut the envelope, drew out the folded sheets, spread them, and began to read.

It was, she saw at once, what she had expected since learning from the postmark that Clare was in the city. An extravagantly phrased wish to see her again. Well, she needn't and wouldn't, Irene told herself, accede to that. Nor would she assist Clare to realize her foolish desire to return for a moment to that life which long ago, and of her own choice, she had left behind her.

She ran through the letter, puzzling out, as best she could, the carelessly formed words or making instinctive guesses at them.

". . . For I am lonely, so lonely . . . cannot help longing to be with you again, as I have never longed for anything before; and I have wanted many things in my life. . . . You can't know how in this pale life of mine I am all the time seeing the bright pictures of that other that I once thought I was glad to be free of. . . . It's like an ache, a pain that never ceases. . . ." Sheets upon thin sheets of it. And ending finally with, "and it's your fault, 'Rene dear. At least partly. For I wouldn't now, perhaps, have this terrible, this wild desire if I hadn't seen you that time in Chicago. . . ."

Brilliant red patches flamed in Irene Redfield's warm olive cheeks.

"That time in Chicago." The words stood out from among the many paragraphs of other words, bringing with them a clear, sharp remembrance, in which even now, after two years, humiliation, resentment, and rage were mingled.

TWO

This is what Irene Redfield remembered.

Chicago. August. A brilliant day, hot, with a brutal staring sun pouring down rays that were like molten rain. A day on which the very outlines of the buildings shuddered as if in protest at the heat. Quivering lines sprang up from baked pavements and wriggled along the shining car-tracks. The automobiles parked at the kerbs were a dancing blaze, and the glass of the shop-windows threw out a blinding radiance. Sharp particles of dust rose from the burning sidewalks, stinging the seared or dripping skins of wilting pedestrians. What small breeze there was seemed like the breath of a flame fanned by slow bellows.

It was on that day of all others that Irene set out to shop for the things which she had promised to take home from Chicago to her two small sons, Brian junior and Theodore. Characteristically, she had put it off until only a few crowded days remained of her long visit. And only this sweltering one was free of engagements till the evening.

Without too much trouble she had got the mechanical aeroplane for Junior. But the drawing-book, for which Ted had so gravely and insistently given her precise directions, had sent her in and out of five shops without success.

It was while she was on her way to a sixth place that right before her smarting eyes a man toppled over and became an inert crumpled heap on the scorching cement. About the lifeless figure a little crowd gathered. Was the man dead, or only faint? someone asked her. But Irene didn't know and didn't try to discover. She edged her way out of the increasing crowd, feeling disagreeably damp and sticky and soiled from contact with so many sweating bodies.

For a moment she stood fanning herself and dabbing at her moist face with an inadequate scrap of handkerchief. Suddenly she was aware that the whole street had a wobbly look, and realized that she was about to faint. With a quick perception of the need for immediate safety, she lifted a wavering hand in the direction of a cab parked directly in front of her. The perspiring driver jumped out and guided her to his car. He helped, almost lifted her in. She sank down on the hot leather seat.

For a minute her thoughts were nebulous. They cleared.

"I guess," she told her Samaritan,[1] "it's tea I need. On a roof somewhere."

"The Drayton, ma'am?" he suggested. "They do say as how it's always a breeze up there."

"Thank you. I think the Drayton'll do nicely," she told him.

There was that little grating sound of the clutch being slipped in as the man put the car in gear and slid deftly out into the boiling traffic. Reviving under the warm breeze stirred up by the moving cab, Irene made some small attempts to repair the damage that the heat and crowds had done to her appearance.

All too soon the rattling vehicle shot towards the sidewalk and stood still. The driver sprang out and opened the door before the hotel's decorated attendant could reach it. She got out, and thanking him smilingly as well as in a more substantial manner for his kind helpfulness and understanding, went in through the Drayton's wide doors.

Stepping out of the elevator that had brought her to the roof, she was led to a table just in front of a long window whose gently moving curtains suggested a cool breeze. It was, she thought, like being wafted upward on a magic carpet to another world, pleasant, quiet, and strangely remote from the sizzling one that she had left below.

The tea, when it came, was all that she had desired and expected. In fact, so much was it what she had desired and expected that after the first deep cooling drink she was able to forget it, only now and then sipping, a little absently, from the tall green glass, while she surveyed the room about her or looked out over some lower buildings at the bright unstirred blue of the lake reaching away to an undetected horizon.

She had been gazing down for some time at the specks of cars and people creeping about in streets, and thinking how silly they looked, when on taking up her glass she was surprised to find it empty at last. She asked for more tea and while she waited, began to recall the happenings of the day and to wonder what she was to do about Ted and his book. Why was it that almost invariably he wanted something that was difficult or impossible to get? Like his father. For ever wanting something that he couldn't have.

Presently there were voices, a man's booming one

and a woman's slightly husky. A waiter passed her, followed by a sweetly scented woman in a fluttering dress of green chiffon whose mingled pattern of narcissuses, jonquils, and hyacinths was a reminder of pleasantly chill spring days. Behind her there was a man, very red in the face, who was mopping his neck and forehead with a big crumpled handkerchief.

"Oh dear!" Irene groaned, rasped by annoyance, for after a little discussion and commotion they had stopped at the very next table. She had been alone there at the window and it had been so satisfyingly quiet. Now, of course, they would chatter.

But no. Only the woman sat down. The man remained standing, abstractedly pinching the knot of his bright blue tie. Across the small space that separated the two tables his voice carried clearly.

"See you later, then," he declared, looking down at the woman. There was pleasure in his tones and a smile on his face.

His companion's lips parted in some answer, but her words were blurred by the little intervening distance and the medley of noises floating up from the streets below. They didn't reach Irene. But she noted the peculiar caressing smile that accompanied them.

The man said: "Well, I suppose I'd better," and smiled again, and said good bye, and left.

An attractive-looking woman, was Irene's opinion, with those dark, almost black, eyes and that wide mouth like a scarlet flower against the ivory of her skin. Nice clothes too, just right for the weather, thin and cool without being mussy, as summer things were so apt to be.

A waiter was taking her order. Irene saw her smile up at him as she murmured something—thanks, maybe. It was an odd sort of smile. Irene couldn't quite define it, but she was sure that she would have classed it, coming from another woman, as being just a shade too provocative for a waiter. About this one, however, there was something that made her hesitate to name it that. A certain impression of assurance, perhaps.

The waiter came back with the order. Irene watched her spread out her napkin, saw the silver spoon in the white hand slit the dull gold of the melon. Then, conscious that she had been staring, she looked quickly away.

Her mind returned to her own affairs. She had settled, definitely, the problem of the proper one of two frocks for the bridge party that night, in rooms whose atmosphere would be so thick and hot that every breath would be like breathing soup. The dress decided, her thoughts had gone back to the snag of Ted's book, her unseeing eyes far away on the lake, when by some sixth sense she was acutely aware that someone was watching her.

Very slowly she looked around, and into the dark eyes of the woman in the green frock at the next table. But she evidently failed to realize that such intense interest as she was showing might be embarrassing, and continued to stare. Her demeanour was that of one who with utmost singleness of mind and purpose was determined to impress firmly and accurately each detail of Irene's features upon her memory for all time, nor showed the slightest trace of disconcertment at having been detected in her steady scrutiny.

Instead, it was Irene who was put out. Feeling her colour heighten under the continued inspection, she slid her eyes down. What, she wondered, could be the reason for such persistent attention? Had she, in her haste in the taxi, put her hat on backwards? Guardedly she felt at it. No. Perhaps there was a streak of powder somewhere on her face. She made a quick pass over it with her handkerchief. Something wrong with her dress? She shot a glance over it. Perfectly all right. *What* was it?

Again she looked up, and for a moment her brown

eyes politely returned the stare of the other's black ones, which never for an instant fell or wavered. Irene made a little mental shrug. Oh well, let her look! She tried to treat the woman and her watching with indifference, but she couldn't. All her efforts to ignore her, it, were futile. She stole another glance. Still looking. What strange languorous eyes she had!

And gradually there rose in Irene a small inner disturbance, odious and hatefully familiar. She laughed softly, but her eyes flashed.

Did that woman, could that woman, somehow know that here before her very eyes on the roof of the Drayton sat a Negro?

Absurd! Impossible! White people were so stupid about such things for all that they usually asserted that they were able to tell; and by the most ridiculous means, finger-nails, palms of hands, shapes of ears, teeth, and other equally silly rot.[2] They always took her for an Italian, a Spaniard, a Mexican, or a gipsy. Never, when she was alone, had they even remotely seemed to suspect that she was a Negro. No, the woman sitting there staring at her couldn't possibly know.

Nevertheless, Irene felt, in turn, anger, scorn, and fear slide over her. It wasn't that she was ashamed of being a Negro, or even of having it declared. It was the idea of being ejected from any place, even in the polite and tactful way in which the Drayton would probably do it, that disturbed her.

But she looked, boldly this time, back into the eyes still frankly intent upon her. They did not seem to her hostile or resentful. Rather, Irene had the feeling that they were ready to smile if she would. Nonsense, of course. The feeling passed, and she turned away with the firm intention of keeping her gaze on the lake, the roofs of the buildings across the way, the sky, anywhere but on that annoying woman. Almost immediately, however, her eyes were back again. In the midst of her fog of uneasiness she had been seized by a desire to outstare the rude observer. Suppose the woman did know or suspect her race. She couldn't prove it.

Suddenly her small fright increased. Her neighbour had risen and was coming towards her. What was going to happen now?

"Pardon me," the woman said pleasantly, "but I think I know you." Her slightly husky voice held a dubious note.

Looking up at her, Irene's suspicions and fears vanished. There was no mistaking the friendliness of that smile or resisting its charm. Instantly she surrendered to it and smiled too, as she said: "I'm afraid you're mistaken."

"Why, of course, I know you!" the other exclaimed. "Don't tell me you're not Irene Westover. Or do they still call you 'Rene?"

In the brief second before her answer, Irene tried vainly to recall where and when this woman could have known her. There, in Chicago. And before her marriage. That much was plain. High school? College? Y.W.C.A. committees? High school, most likely. What white girls had she known well enough to have been familiarly addressed as 'Rene by them? The woman before her didn't fit her memory of any of them. Who was she?

"Yes, I'm Irene Westover. And though nobody calls me 'Rene any more, it's good to hear the name again. And you—" She hesitated, ashamed that she could not remember, and hoping that the sentence would be finished for her.

"Don't you know me? Not really, 'Rene?"

"I'm sorry, but just at the minute I can't seem to place you."

Irene studied the lovely creature standing beside her for some clue to her identity. Who could she be? Where and when had they met? And through her perplexity there came the thought that the trick which her memory had played her was for some reason more gratifying than disappointing to her old acquaintance, that she didn't mind not being recognized.

And, too, Irene felt that she was just about to remember her. For about the woman was some quality, an intangible something, too vague to define, too remote to seize, but which was, to Irene Redfield, very familiar. And that voice. Surely she'd heard those husky tones somewhere before. Perhaps before time, contact, or something had been at them, making them into a voice remotely suggesting England. Ah! Could it have been in Europe that they had met? 'Rene. No.

"Perhaps," Irene began, "you—"

The woman laughed, a lovely laugh, a small sequence of notes that was like a trill and also like the ringing of a delicate bell fashioned of a precious metal, a tinkling.

Irene drew a quick sharp breath. "Clare!" she exclaimed, "not really Clare Kendry?"

So great was her astonishment that she had started to rise.

"No, no, don't get up," Clare Kendry commanded, and sat down herself. "You've simply got to stay and talk. We'll have something more. Tea? Fancy meeting you here! It's simply too, too lucky!"

"It's awfully surprising," Irene told her, and, seeing the change in Clare's smile, knew that she had revealed a corner of her own thoughts. But she only said: "I'd never in this world have known you if you hadn't laughed. You are changed, you know. And yet, in a way, you're just the same."

"Perhaps," Clare replied. "Oh, just a second."

She gave her attention to the waiter at her side. "M-mm, let's see. Two teas. And bring some cigarettes. Y-es, they'll be all right. Thanks." Again that odd upward smile. Now, Irene was sure that it was too provocative for a waiter.

While Clare had been giving the order, Irene made a rapid mental calculation. It must be, she figured, all of twelve years since she, or anybody that she knew, had laid eyes on Clare Kendry.

After her father's death she'd gone to live with some relatives, aunts or cousins two or three times removed, over on the west side: relatives that nobody had known the Kendrys' possessed until they had turned up at the funeral and taken Clare away with them.

For about a year or more afterwards she would appear occasionally among her old friends and acquaintances on the south side for short little visits that were, they understood, always stolen from the endless domestic tasks in her new home. With each succeeding one she was taller, shabbier, and more belligerently sensitive. And each time the look on her face was more resentful and brooding. "I'm worried about Clare, she seems so unhappy," Irene remembered her mother saying. The visits dwindled, becoming shorter, fewer, and further apart until at last they ceased.

Irene's father, who had been fond of Bob Kendry, made a special trip over to the west side about two months after the last time Clare had been to see them and returned with the bare information that he had seen the relatives and that Clare had disappeared. What else he had confided to her mother, in the privacy of their own room, Irene didn't know.

But she had had something more than a vague suspicion of its nature. For there had been rumours. Rumours that were, to girls of eighteen and nineteen years, interesting and exciting.

There was the one about Clare Kendry's having been seen at the dinner hour in a fashionable hotel in company with another woman and two men, all of them white. And *dressed*! And there was another which told of her driving in Lincoln Park with a man, unmistakably white, and evidently rich. Packard limousine, chauffeur in livery, and all that. There had been others whose context Irene could no longer recollect, but all pointing in the same glamorous direction.

And she could remember quite vividly how, when they used to repeat and discuss these tantalizing stories about Clare, the girls would always look knowingly at one another and then, with little excited giggles, drag away their eager shining eyes and say with lurking undertones of regret or disbelief some such thing as: "Oh, well, maybe she's got a job or something," or "After all, it mayn't have been Clare," or "You can't believe all you hear."

And always some girl, more matter-of-fact or more frankly malicious than the rest, would declare: "Of course it was Clare! Ruth said it was and so did Frank, and they certainly know her when they see her as well as we do." And someone else would say: "Yes, you can bet it was Clare all right." And then they would all join in asserting that there could be no mistake about it's having been Clare, and that such circumstances could mean only one thing. Working indeed! People didn't take their servants to the Shelby for dinner. Certainly not all dressed up like that. There would follow insincere regrets, and somebody would say: "Poor girl, I suppose it's true enough, but what can you expect. Look at her father. And her mother, they say, would have run away if she hadn't died. Besides, Clare always had a—a—having way with her."

Precisely that! The words came to Irene as she sat

there on the Drayton roof, facing Clare Kendry. "A having way." Well, Irene acknowledged, judging from her appearance and manner, Clare seemed certainly to have succeeded in having a few of the things that she wanted.

It was, Irene repeated, after the interval of the waiter, a great surprise and a very pleasant one to see Clare again after all those years, twelve at least.

"Why, Clare, you're the last person in the world I'd have expected to run into. I guess that's why I didn't know you."

Clare answered gravely: "Yes. It is twelve years. But I'm not surprised to see you, 'Rene. That is, not so very. In fact, ever since I've been here, I've more or less hoped that I should, or someone. Preferably you, though. Still, I imagine that's because I've thought of you often and often, while you—I'll wager you've never given me a thought."

It was true, of course. After the first speculations and indictments, Clare had gone completely from Irene's thoughts. And from the thoughts of others too—if their conversation was any indication of their thoughts.

Besides, Clare had never been exactly one of the group, just as she'd never been merely the janitor's daughter, but the daughter of Mr. Bob Kendry, who, it was true, was a janitor, but who also, it seemed, had been in college with some of their fathers. Just how or why he happened to be a janitor, and a very inefficient one at that, they none of them quite knew. One of Irene's brothers, who had put the question to their father, had been told: "That's something that doesn't concern you," and given him the advice to be careful not to end in the same manner as "poor Bob."

No, Irene hadn't thought of Clare Kendry. Her own life had been too crowded. So, she supposed, had the lives of other people. She defended her—their— forgetfulness. "You know how it is. Everybody's so busy. People leave, drop out, maybe for a little while there's talk about them, or questions; then, gradually they're forgotten."

"Yes, that's natural," Clare agreed. And what, she inquired, had they said of her for that little while at the beginning before they'd forgotten her altogether?

Irene looked away. She felt the telltale colour rising in her cheeks. "You can't," she evaded, "expect me to remember trifles like that over twelve years of marriages, births, deaths, and the war."

There followed that trill of notes that was Clare Kendry's laugh, small and clear and the very essence of mockery.

"Oh, 'Rene!" she cried, "of course you remember! But I won't make you tell me, because I know just as well as if I'd been there and heard every unkind word. Oh, I know, I know. Frank Danton saw me in the Shelby one night. Don't tell me he didn't broadcast that, and with embroidery. Others may have seen me at other times. I don't know. But once I met Margaret Hammer in Marshall Field's.³ I'd have spoken, was on the very point of doing it, but she cut me dead. My dear 'Rene, I assure you that from the way she looked through me, even I was uncertain whether I was actually there in the flesh or not. I remember it clearly, too clearly. It was that very thing which, in a way, finally decided me not to go out and see you one last time before I went away to stay. Somehow, good as all of you, the whole family, had always been to the poor forlorn child that was me, I felt I shouldn't be able to bear that. I mean if any of you, your mother or the boys or— Oh, well, I just felt I'd rather not know it if you did. And so I stayed away. Silly, I suppose. Sometimes I've been sorry I didn't go."

Irene wondered if it was tears that made Clare's eyes so luminous.

"And now 'Rene, I want to hear all about you and everybody and everything. You're married, I s'pose?"

Irene nodded.

"Yes," Clare said knowingly, "you would be. Tell me about it."

And so for an hour or more they had sat there smoking and drinking tea and filling in the gap of twelve years with talk. That is, Irene did. She told Clare about her marriage and removal to New York, about her husband, and about her two sons, who were having their first experience of being separated from their parents at a summer camp, about her mother's death, about the marriages of her two brothers. She told of the marriages, births and deaths in other families that Clare had known, opening up, for her, new vistas on the lives of old friends and acquaintances.

Clare drank it all in, these things which for so long she had wanted to know and hadn't been able to learn. She sat motionless, her bright lips slightly parted, her whole face lit by the radiance of her happy eyes. Now and then she put a question, but for the most part she was silent.

Somewhere outside, a clock struck. Brought back to the present, Irene looked down at her watch and exclaimed: "Oh, I must go, Clare!"

A moment passed during which she was the prey of uneasiness. It had suddenly occurred to her that she hadn't asked Clare anything about her own life and that she had a very definite unwillingness to do so. And she was quite well aware of the reason for that reluctance. But, she asked herself, wouldn't it, all things considered, be the kindest thing not to ask? If things with Clare were as she—as they all—had suspected, wouldn't it be more tactful to seem to forget to inquire how she had spent those twelve years?

If? It was that "if" which bothered her. It might be, it might just be, in spite of all gossip and even appearances to the contrary, that there was nothing, had been nothing, that couldn't be simply and innocently explained. Appearances, she knew now, had a way sometimes of not fitting facts, and if Clare hadn't— Well, if they had all been wrong, then certainly she ought to express some interest in what had happened to her. It would seem queer and rude if she didn't. But how was she to know? There was, she at last decided, no way; so she merely said again: "I must go, Clare."

"Please, not so soon, 'Rene," Clare begged, not moving.

Irene thought: "She's really almost too good-looking. It's hardly any wonder that she—"

"And now, 'Rene dear, that I've found you, I mean to see lots and lots of you. We're here for a month at least. Jack, that's my husband, is here on business. Poor dear! in this heat. Isn't it beastly? Come to dinner with us tonight, won't you?" And she gave Irene a curious little sidelong glance and a sly, ironical smile peeped out on her full red lips, as if she had been in the secret of the other's thoughts and was mocking her.

Irene was conscious of a sharp intake of breath, but whether it was relief or chagrin that she felt, she herself could not have told. She said hastily: "I'm afraid I can't, Clare. I'm filled up. Dinner and bridge. I'm so sorry."

"Come tomorrow instead, to tea," Clare insisted. "Then you'll see Margery—she's just ten—and Jack too, maybe, if he hasn't got an appointment or something."

From Irene came an uneasy little laugh. She had an engagement for tomorrow also and she was afraid that Clare would not believe it. Suddenly, now, that possibility disturbed her. Therefore it was with a half-vexed feeling at the sense of undeserved guilt that had come upon her that she explained that it wouldn't be possible because she wouldn't be free for tea, or for luncheon or dinner either. "And the next day's Friday when I'll be going away for the weekend, Idlewild,[4] you know. It's quite the thing now." And then she had an inspiration.

"Clare!" she exclaimed, "why don't you come up

with me? Our place is probably full up—Jim's wife has a way of collecting mobs of the most impossible people—but we can always manage to find room for one more. And you'll see absolutely everybody."

In the very moment of giving the invitation she regretted it. What a foolish, what an idiotic impulse to have given way to! She groaned inwardly as she thought of the endless explanations in which it would involve her, of the curiosity, and the talk, and the lifted eyebrows. It wasn't she assured herself, that she was a snob, that she cared greatly for the petty restrictions and distinctions with which what called itself Negro society chose to hedge itself about; but that she had a natural and deeply rooted aversion to the kind of front-page notoriety that Clare Kendry's presence in Idlewild, as her guest, would expose her to. And here she was, perversely and against all reason, inviting her.

But Clare shook her head. "Really, I'd love to, 'Rene," she said, a little mournfully. "There's nothing I'd like better. But I couldn't. I mustn't, you see. It wouldn't do at all. I'm sure you understand. I'm simply crazy to go, but I can't." The dark eyes glistened and there was a suspicion of a quaver in the husky voice. "And believe me, 'Rene, I do thank you for asking me. Don't think I've entirely forgotten just what it would mean for you if I went. That is, if you still care about such things."

All indication of tears had gone from her eyes and voice, and Irene Redfield, searching her face, had an offended feeling that behind what was now only an ivory mask lurked a scornful amusement. She looked away, at the wall far beyond Clare. Well, she deserved it, for, as she acknowledged to herself, she *was* relieved. And for the very reason at which Clare had hinted. The fact that Clare had guessed her perturbation did not, however, in any degree lessen that relief. She was annoyed at having been detected in what might seem to be an insincerity; but that was all.

The waiter came with Clare's change. Irene reminded herself that she ought immediately to go. But she didn't move.

The truth was, she was curious. There were things that she wanted to ask Clare Kendry. She wished to find out about this hazardous business of "passing," this breaking away from all that was familiar and friendly to take one's chance in another environment, not entirely strange, perhaps, but certainly not entirely friendly. What, for example, one did about background, how one accounted for oneself. And how one felt when one came into contact with other Negroes. But she couldn't. She was unable to think of a single question that in its context or its phrasing was not too frankly curious, if not actually impertinent.

As if aware of her desire and her hesitation, Clare remarked, thoughtfully: "You know, 'Rene, I've often wondered why more coloured girls, girls like you and Margaret Hammer and Esther Dawson and—oh, lots of others—never 'passed' over. It's such a frightfully easy thing to do. If one's the type, all that's needed is a little nerve."

"What about background? Family, I mean. Surely you can't just drop down on people from nowhere and expect them to receive you with open arms, can you?"

"Almost," Clare asserted. "You'd be surprised, 'Rene, how much easier that is with white people than with us. Maybe because there are so many more of them, or maybe because they are secure and so don't have to bother. I've never quite decided."

Irene was inclined to be incredulous. "You mean that you didn't have to explain where you came from? It seems impossible."

Clare cast a glance of repressed amusement across the table at her. "As a matter of fact, I didn't. Though I suppose under any other circumstances I might have had to provide some plausible tale to account for myself. I've a good imagination, so I'm sure I could have done it quite creditably, and credibly. But it wasn't necessary. There were my aunts, you see, respectable and authentic enough for anything or anybody."

"I see. They were 'passing' too."

"No. They weren't. They were white."

"Oh!" And in the next instant it came back to Irene that she had heard this mentioned before; by her father, or, more likely, her mother. They were Bob Kendry's aunts. He had been a son of their brother's, on the left hand. A wild oat.

"They were nice old ladies," Clare explained, "very religious and as poor as church mice. That adored brother of theirs, my grandfather, got through every penny they had after he'd finished his own little bit."

Clare paused in her narrative to light another cigarette. Her smile, her expression, Irene noticed, was faintly resentful.

"Being good Christians," she continued, "when dad came to his tipsy end, they did their duty and gave me a home of sorts. I was, it was true, expected to earn my keep by doing all the housework and most of the washing. But do you realize, 'Rene, that if it hadn't been for them, I shouldn't have had a home in the world?"

Irene's nod and little murmur were comprehensive, understanding.

Clare made a small mischievous grimace and proceeded. "Besides, to their notion, hard labour was good for me. I had Negro blood[5] and they belonged to the generation that had written and read long articles headed: 'Will the Blacks Work?' Too, they weren't quite sure that the good God hadn't intended the sons and daughters of Ham[6] to sweat because he had poked fun at old man Noah once when he had taken a drop too much. I remember the aunts telling me that that old drunkard had cursed Ham and his sons for all time."

Irene laughed. But Clare remained quite serious.

"It was more than a joke, I assure you, 'Rene. It was a hard life for a girl of sixteen. Still, I had a roof over my head, and food, and clothes—such as they were. And there were the Scriptures, and talks on morals and thrift and industry and the loving-kindness of the good Lord."

"Have you ever stopped to think, Clare," Irene demanded, "how much unhappiness and downright cruelty are laid to the loving-kindness of the Lord? And always by His most ardent followers, it seems."

"Have I?" Clare exclaimed. "It, they, made me what I am today. For, of course, I was determined to get away, to be a person and not a charity or a problem, or even a daughter of the indiscreet Ham. Then, too, I wanted things. I knew I wasn't bad-looking and that I could 'pass.' You can't know, 'Rene, how, when I used to go over to the south side, I used almost to hate all of you. You had all the things I wanted and never had had. It made me all the more determined to get them, and others. Do you, can you understand what I felt?"

She looked up with a pointed and appealing effect, and, evidently finding the sympathetic expression on Irene's face sufficient answer, went on. "The aunts were queer. For all their Bibles and praying and ranting about honesty, they didn't want anyone to know that their darling brother had seduced—ruined, they called it—a Negro girl. They could excuse the ruin, but they couldn't forgive the tar-brush.[7] They forbade me to mention Negroes to the neighbours, or even to mention the south side. You may be sure that I didn't. I'll bet they were good and sorry afterwards."

She laughed and the ringing bells in her laugh had a hard metallic sound.

"When the chance to get away came, that omission was of great value to me. When Jack, a schoolboy acquaintance of some people in the neighbourhood, turned up from South America with untold gold, there was no one to tell him that I was coloured, and

many to tell him about the severity and the religious-
ness of Aunt Grace and Aunt Edna. You can guess the
rest. After he came, I stopped slipping off to the south
side and slipped off to meet him instead. I couldn't
manage both. In the end I had no great difficulty in
convincing him that it was useless to talk marriage to
the aunts. So on the day that I was eighteen, we went
off and were married. So that's that. Nothing could
have been easier."

"Yes, I do see that for you it was easy enough. By
the way! I wonder why they didn't tell father that you
were married. He went over to find out about you
when you stopped coming over to see us. I'm sure
they didn't tell him. Not that you were married."

Clare Kendry's eyes were bright with tears that
didn't fall. "Oh, how lovely! To have cared enough
about me to do that. The dear sweet man! Well, they
couldn't tell him because they didn't know it. I took
care of that, for I couldn't be sure that those con-
sciences of theirs wouldn't begin to work on them afterwards and make them let the cat out of the bag.
The old things probably thought I was living in sin,
wherever I was. And it would be about what they expected."

An amused smile lit the lovely face for the smallest
fraction of a second. After a little silence she said

soberly: "But I'm sorry if they told your father so. That was something I hadn't counted on."

"I'm not sure that they did," Irene told her. "He didn't say so, anyway."

"He wouldn't, 'Rene dear. Not your father."

"Thanks. I'm sure he wouldn't."

"But you've never answered my question. Tell me, honestly, haven't you ever thought of 'passing'?"

Irene answered promptly: "No. Why should I?" And so disdainful was her voice and manner that Clare's face flushed and her eyes glinted. Irene hastened to add: "You see, Clare, I've everything I want. Except, perhaps, a little more money."

At that Clare laughed, her spark of anger vanished as quickly as it had appeared. "Of course," she declared, "that's what everybody wants, just a little more money, even the people who have it. And I must say I don't blame them. Money's awfully nice to have. In fact, all things considered, I think, 'Rene, that it's even worth the price."

Irene could only shrug her shoulders. Her reason partly agreed, her instinct wholly rebelled. And she could not say why. And though conscious that if she didn't hurry away, she was going to be late to dinner, she still lingered. It was as if the woman sitting on the other side of the table, a girl that she had known, who had done this rather dangerous and, to Irene Redfield, abhorrent thing successfully and had announced herself well satisfied, had for her a fascination, strange and compelling.

Clare Kendry was still leaning back in the tall chair, her sloping shoulders against the carved top. She sat with an air of indifferent assurance, as if arranged for, desired. About her clung that dim suggestion of polite insolence with which a few women are born and which some acquire with the coming of riches or importance.

Clare, it gave Irene a little prick of satisfaction to recall, hadn't got that by passing herself off as white. She herself had always had it.

Just as she'd always had that pale gold hair, which, unsheared still, was drawn loosely back from a broad brow, partly hidden by the small close hat. Her lips, painted a brilliant geranium-red, were sweet and sensitive and a little obstinate. A tempting mouth. The face across the forehead and cheeks was a trifle too wide, but the ivory skin had a peculiar soft lustre. And the eyes were magnificent! dark, sometimes absolutely black, always luminous, and set in long, black lashes. Arresting eyes, slow and mesmeric, and with, for all their warmth, something withdrawn and secret about them.

Ah! Surely! They were Negro eyes! mysterious and concealing. And set in that ivory face under that bright hair, there was about them something exotic.

Yes, Clare Kendry's loveliness was absolute, beyond challenge, thanks to those eyes which her grandmother and later her mother and father had given her.

Into those eyes there came a smile and over Irene the sense of being petted and caressed. She smiled back.

"Maybe," Clare suggested, "you can come Monday, if you're back. Or, if you're not, then Tuesday."

With a small regretful sigh, Irene informed Clare that she was afraid she wouldn't be back by Monday and that she was sure she had dozens of things for Tuesday, and that she was leaving Wednesday. It might be, however, that she could get out of something Tuesday.

"Oh, do try. Do put somebody else off. The others can see you any time, while I—Why, I may never see you again! Think of that, 'Rene! You'll have to come. You'll simply have to! I'll never forgive you if you don't."

At that moment it seemed a dreadful thing to think of never seeing Clare Kendry again. Standing there under the appeal, the caress, of her eyes, Irene had the desire, the hope, that this parting wouldn't be the last.

"I'll try, Clare," she promised gently. "I'll call you—or will you call me?"

"I think, perhaps, I'd better call you. Your father's in the book, I know, and the address is the same. Sixty-four eighteen. Some memory, what? Now remember, I'm going to expect you. You've got to be able to come."

Again that peculiar mellowing smile.

"I'll do my best, Clare."

Irene gathered up her gloves and bag. They stood up. She put out her hand. Clare took and held it.

"It has been nice seeing you again, Clare. How pleased and glad father'll be to hear about you!"

"Until Tuesday, then," Clare Kendry replied. "I'll spend every minute of the time from now on looking forward to seeing you again. Good-bye, 'Rene dear. My love to your father, and this kiss for him."

———

The sun had gone from overhead, but the streets were still like fiery furnaces. The languid breeze was still hot. And the scurrying people looked even more wilted than before Irene had fled from their contact.

Crossing the avenue in the heat, far from the coolness of the Drayton's roof, away from the seduction of

Clare Kendry's smile, she was aware of a sense of ir-ritation with herself because she had been pleased and a little flattered at the other's obvious gladness at their meeting.

With her perspiring progress homeward this irrita-tion grew, and she began to wonder just what had pos-sessed her to make her promise to find time, in the crowded days that remained of her visit, to spend an-other afternoon with a woman whose life had so defi-nitely and deliberately diverged from hers; and whom, as had been pointed out, she might never see again.

Why in the world had she made such a promise?

As she went up the steps to her father's house, thinking with what interest and amazement he would listen to her story of the afternoon's encounter, it came to her that Clare had omitted to mention her marriage name. She had referred to her husband as Jack. That was all. Had that, Irene asked herself, been intentional?

Clare had only to pick up the telephone to com-municate with her, or to drop her a card, or to jump into a taxi. But she couldn't reach Clare in any way. Nor could anyone else to whom she might speak of their meeting.

"As if I should!"

Her key turned in the lock. She went in. Her father, it seemed, hadn't come in yet.

Irene decided that she wouldn't, after all, say anything to him about Clare Kendry. She had, she told herself, no inclination to speak of a person who held so low an opinion of her loyalty, or her discretion. And certainly she had no desire or intention of making the slightest effort about Tuesday. Nor any other day for that matter.

She was through with Clare Kendry.

THREE

On Tuesday morning a dome of grey sky rose over the parched city, but the stifling air was not relieved by the silvery mist that seemed to hold a promise of rain, which did not fall.

To Irene Redfield this soft foreboding fog was another reason for doing nothing about seeing Clare Kendry that afternoon.

But she did see her.

The telephone. For hours it had rung like something possessed. Since nine o'clock she had been hearing its insistent jangle. Awhile she was resolute, saying firmly each time: "Not in, Liza, take the message." And each time the servant returned with the information: "It's the same lady, ma'am; she says she'll call again."

But at noon, her nerves frayed and her conscience smiting her at the reproachful look on Liza's ebony face as she withdrew for another denial, Irene weakened.

"Oh, never mind. I'll answer this time, Liza."

"It's her again."

"Hello. . . . Yes."

"It's Clare, 'Rene. . . . Where *have* you been? . . . Can you be here around four? . . . What? . . . But, 'Rene, you promised! Just for a little while. . . . You can if you want to. . . . I am *so* disappointed. I had counted so on seeing you. . . . Please be nice and come. Only for a minute. I'm sure you can manage it if you try. . . . I won't beg you to stay. . . . Yes. . . . I'm going to expect you . . . It's the Morgan . . . Oh, yes! The name's Bellew, Mrs. John Bellew. . . . About four, then. . . . I'll be so happy to see you! . . . Goodbye."

"Damn!"

Irene hung up the receiver with an emphatic bang, her thoughts immediately filled with self-reproach. She'd done it again. Allowed Clare Kendry to persuade her into promising to do something for which she had neither time nor any special desire. What was it about Clare's voice that was so appealing, so very seductive?

Clare met her in the hall with a kiss. She said: "You're good to come, 'Rene. But, then, you always were nice to me." And under her potent smile a part of Irene's annoyance with herself fled. She was even a little glad that she had come.

Clare led the way, stepping lightly, towards a room whose door was standing partly open, saying: "There's a surprise. It's a real party. See."

Entering, Irene found herself in a sitting-room, large and high, at whose windows hung startling blue draperies which triumphantly dragged attention from the gloomy chocolate-coloured furniture. And Clare was wearing a thin floating dress of the same shade of blue, which suited her and the rather difficult room to perfection.

For a minute Irene thought the room was empty, but turning her head, she discovered, sunk deep in the cushions of a huge sofa, a woman staring up at her with such intense concentration that her eyelids were drawn as though the strain of that upward glance had paralysed them. At first Irene took her to be a stranger, but in the next instant she said in an unsympathetic, almost harsh voice: "And how are you, Gertrude?"

The woman nodded and forced a smile to her pouting lips. "I'm all right," she replied. "And you're just the same, Irene. Not changed a bit."

"Thank you." Irene responded, as she chose a seat. She was thinking: "Great goodness! Two of them."

For Gertrude too had married a white man, though it couldn't be truthfully said that she was "passing." Her husband—what was his name?—had been in school with her and had been quite well aware, as had his family and most of his friends, that she was a Negro. It hadn't, Irene knew, seemed to matter to him then. Did it now, she wondered? Had Fred—Fred Martin, that was it—had he ever regretted his marriage because of Gertrude's race? Had Gertrude?

Turning to Gertrude, Irene asked: "And Fred, how is he? It's unmentionable years since I've seen him."

"Oh, he's all right," Gertrude answered briefly.

For a full minute no one spoke. Finally out of the oppressive little silence Clare's voice came pleasantly, conversationally: "We'll have tea right away. I know that you can't stay long, 'Rene. And I'm so sorry you won't see Margery. We went up the lake over the week end to see some of Jack's people, just out of Milwaukee. Margery wanted to stay with the children. It seemed a shame not to let her, especially since it's so hot in town. But I'm expecting Jack any second."

Irene said briefly: "That's nice."

Gertrude remained silent. She was, it was plain, a little ill at ease. And her presence there annoyed Irene, roused in her a defensive and resentful feeling for which she had at the moment no explanation. But it did seem to her odd that the woman that Clare was now should have invited the woman that Gertrude was. Still, of course, Clare couldn't have known. Twelve years since they had met.

Later, when she examined her feeling of annoyance, Irene admitted, a shade reluctantly, that it arose from a feeling of being outnumbered, a sense of aloneness, in her adherence to her own class and kind; not merely in the great thing of marriage, but in the whole pattern of her life as well.

Clare spoke again, this time at length. Her talk was of the change that Chicago presented to her after her long absence in European cities. Yes, she said in reply to some question from Gertrude, she'd been back to America a time or two, but only as far as New York and Philadelphia, and once she had spent a few days in Washington. John Bellew, who, it appeared, was some sort of international banking agent, hadn't particularly wanted her to come with him on this trip, but as soon as she had learned that it would probably take him as far as Chicago, she made up her mind to come anyway.

"I simply had to. And after I once got here, I was determined to see someone I knew and find out what had happened to everybody. I didn't quite see how I was going to manage it, but I meant to. Somehow. I'd just about decided to take a chance and go out to your house, 'Rene, or call up and arrange a meeting, when I ran into you. What luck!"

Irene agreed that it was luck. "It's the first time I've been home for five years, and now I'm about to leave. A week later and I'd have been gone. And how in the world did you find Gertrude?"

"In the book. I remembered about Fred. His father still has the meat market."

"Oh, yes," said Irene, who had only remembered it as Clare had spoken, "on Cottage Grove near—"

Gertrude broke in. "No. It's moved. We're on Maryland Avenue—used to be Jackson—now. Near Sixty-third Street. And the market's Fred's. His name's the same as his father's."

Gertrude, Irene thought, looked as if her husband might be a butcher. There was left of her youthful prettiness, which had been so much admired in their high-school days, no trace. She had grown broad, fat almost, and though there were no lines on her large white face, its very smoothness was somehow prematurely ageing. Her black hair was clipt, and by some unfortunate means all the live curliness had gone from it. Her over-trimmed Georgette *crêpe* dress was too short and showed an appalling amount of leg, stout legs in sleazy stockings of a vivid rose-beige shade. Her plump hands wee newly and not too competently manicured—for the occasion, probably. And she wasn't smoking.

Clare said—and Irene fancied that her husky voice held a slight edge—"Before you came, Irene, Gertrude was telling me about her two boys. Twins. Think of it! Isn't it too marvellous for words?"

Irene felt a warmness creeping into her cheeks. Uncanny, the way Clare could divine what one was thinking. She was a little put out, but her manner was entirely easy as she said: "That is nice. I've two boys myself, Gertrude. Not twins, though. It seems that Clare's rather behind, doesn't it?"

Gertrude, however, wasn't sure that Clare hadn't the best of it. "She's got a girl. I wanted a girl. So did Fred."

"Isn't that a bit unusual?" Irene asked. "Most men want sons. Egotism, I suppose."

"Well, Fred didn't."

The tea-things had been placed on a low table at Clare's side. She gave them her attention now, pouring the rich amber fluid from the tall glass pitcher into stately slim glasses, which she handed to her guests, and then offered them lemon or cream and tiny sandwiches or cakes.

After taking up her own glass she informed them: "No, I have no boys and I don't think I'll ever have any. I'm afraid. I nearly died of terror the whole nine months before Margery was born for fear that she might be dark.[1] Thank goodness, she turned out all right. But I'll never risk it again. Never! The strain is simply too—too hellish."

Gertrude Martin nodded in complete comprehension.

This time it was Irene who said nothing.

"You don't have to tell me!" Gertrude said fervently. "I know what it is all right. Maybe you don't think I wasn't scared to death too. Fred said I was silly, and so did his mother. But, of course, they thought it was just a notion I'd gotten into my head and they blamed it on my condition. They don't know like we do, how it might go way back, and turn out dark no matter what colour the father and mother are."

Perspiration stood out on her forehead. Her narrow eyes rolled first in Clare's, then in Irene's direction. As she talked she waved her heavy hands about.

"No," she went on, "no more for me either. Not even a girl. It's awful the way it skips generations and then pops out. Why, he actually said he didn't care what colour it turned out, if I would only stop worrying about it. But, of course, nobody wants a dark child." Her voice was earnest and she took for granted that her audience was in entire agreement with her.

Irene, whose head had gone up with a quick little jerk, now said in a voice of whose even tones she was proud: "One of my boys is dark."

Gertrude jumped as if she had been shot at. Her eyes goggled. Her mouth flew open. She tried to speak, but could not immediately get the words out. Finally she managed to stammer: "Oh! And your husband, is he—is he—er—dark, too?"

Irene, who was struggling with a flood of feelings, resentment, anger, and contempt, was, however, still able to answer as coolly as if she had not that sense of not belonging to and of despising the company in which she found herself drinking iced tea from tall amber glasses on that hot August afternoon. Her husband, she informed them quietly, couldn't exactly "pass."

At that reply Clare turned on Irene her seductive

caressing smile and remarked a little scoffingly: "I do think that coloured people—we—are too silly about some things. After all, the thing's not important to Irene or hundreds of others. Not awfully, even to you, Gertrude. It's only deserters like me who have to be afraid of freaks of the nature. As my inestimable dad used to say, 'Everything must be paid for.' Now, please one of you tell me what ever happened to Claude Jones. You know, the tall, lanky specimen who used to wear that comical little moustache that the girls used to laugh at so. Like a thin streak of soot. The moustache, I mean."

At that Gertrude shrieked with laughter. "Claude Jones!" and launched into the story of how he was no longer a Negro or a Christian but had become a Jew.

"A Jew!" Clare exclaimed.

"Yes, a Jew. A black Jew,[2] he calls himself. He won't eat ham and goes to the synagogue on Saturday. He's got a beard now as well as a moustache. You'd die laughing if you saw him. He's really too funny for words. Fred says he's crazy and I guess he is. Oh, he's a scream all right, a regular scream!" And she shrieked again.

Clare's laugh tinkled out. "It certainly sounds funny enough. Still, it's his own business. If he gets along better by turning—"

At that, Irene, who was still hugging her unhappy don't-care feeling of rightness, broke in, saying bitingly: "It evidently doesn't occur to either you or Gertrude that he might possibly be sincere in changing his religion. Surely everyone doesn't do everything for gain."

Clare Kendry had no need to search for the full meaning of that utterance. She reddened slightly and retorted seriously: "Yes, I admit that might be possible—his being sincere, I mean. It just didn't happen to occur to me, that's all. I'm surprised," and the seriousness changed to mockery, "that you should have expected it to. Or did you really?"

"You don't, I'm sure, imagine that that is a question that I can answer," Irene told her. "Not here and now."

Gertrude's face expressed complete bewilderment. However, seeing that little smiles had come out on the faces of the two other women and not recognizing them for the smiles of mutual reservations which they were, she smiled too.

Clare began to talk, steering carefully away from anything that might lead towards race or other thorny subjects. It was the most brilliant exhibition of conversational weightlifting that Irene had ever seen. Her words swept over them in charming well-modulated streams. Her laughs tinkled and pealed. Her little stories sparkled.

Irene contributed a bare "Yes" or "No" here and there. Gertrude, a "You don't say!" less frequently.

For a while the illusion of general conversation was nearly perfect. Irene felt her resentment changing gradually to a silent, somewhat grudging admiration.

Clare talked on, her voice, her gestures colouring all she said of wartime in France, of after-the-wartime in Germany, of the excitement at the time of the general strike in England, of dressmakers' openings in Paris, of the new gaiety of Budapest.[3]

But it couldn't last, this verbal feat. Gertrude shifted in her seat and fell to fidgeting with her fingers. Irene, bored at last by all this repetition of the selfsame things that she had read all too often in papers, magazines, and books, set down her glass and collected her bag and handkerchief. She was smoothing out the tan fingers of her gloves preparatory to putting them on when she heard the sound of the outer door being opened and saw Clare spring up with an expression of relief saying: "How lovely! Here's Jack at exactly the right minute. You can't go now, 'Rene dear."

John Bellew came into the room. The first thing that Irene noticed about him was that he was not the man that she had seen with Clare Kendry on the Drayton roof. This man, Clare's husband, was a tallish person, broadly made. His age she guessed to be somewhere between thirty-five and forty. His hair was dark brown and waving, and he had a soft mouth, somewhat womanish, set in an unhealthy-looking dough-coloured face. His steel-grey opaque eyes were very much alive, moving ceaselessly between thick bluish lids. But there was, Irene decided, nothing unusual about him, unless it was an impression of latent physical power.

"Hello, Nig," was his greeting to Clare.

Gertrude who had started slightly, settled back and looked covertly towards Irene, who had caught her lip between her teeth and sat gazing at husband and wife. It was hard to believe that even Clare Kendry would permit this ridiculing of her race by an outsider, though he chanced to be her husband. So he knew, then, that Clare was a Negro? From her talk the other day Irene had understood that he didn't. But how rude, how positively insulting, for him to address her in that way in the presence of guests!

In Clare's eyes, as she presented her husband, was a queer gleam, a jeer, it might be. Irene couldn't define it.

The mechanical professions that attend an introduction over, she inquired: "Did you hear what Jack called me?"

"Yes," Gertrude answered, laughing with a dutiful eagerness.

Irene didn't speak. Her gaze remained level on Clare's smiling face.

The black eyes fluttered down. "Tell them, dear, why you call me that."

The man chuckled, crinkling up his eyes, not, Irene was compelled to acknowledge, unpleasantly. He explained: "Well, you see, it's like this. When we were first married, she was as white as—as—well as white as a lily. But I declare she's gettin' darker and darker. I tell her if she don't look out, she'll wake up one of these days and find she's turned into a nigger."

He roared with laughter. Clare's ringing bell-like laugh joined his. Gertrude after another uneasy shift in her seat added her shrill one. Irene, who had been sitting with lips tightly compressed, cried out: "That's good!" and gave way to gales of laughter. She laughed and laughed and laughed. Tears ran down her cheeks. Her sides ached. Her throat hurt. She laughed on and on and on, long after the others had subsided. Until, catching sight of Clare's face, the need for a more quiet enjoyment of this priceless joke, and for caution, struck her. At once she stopped.

Clare handed her husband his tea and laid her hand on his arm with an affectionate little gesture. Speaking with confidence as well as with amusement, she said: "My goodness, Jack! What difference would it make if, after all these years, you were to find out that I was one or two per cent coloured?"

Bellew put out his hand in a repudiating fling, definite and final. "Oh, no, Nig," he declared, "nothing like that with me. I know you're no nigger, so it's all right. You can get as black as you please as far as I'm concerned, since I know you're no nigger. I draw the line at that. No niggers in my family. Never have been and never will be."

Irene's lips trembled almost uncontrollably, but she made a desperate effort to fight back her disastrous desire to laugh again, and succeeded. Carefully selecting a cigarette from the lacquered box on the tea-table before her, she turned an oblique look on Clare and encountered her peculiar eyes fixed on her with an expression so dark and deep and unfathomable that she had for a short moment the sensation of gazing into the eyes of some creature utterly strange and apart. A faint sense of danger brushed her, like the breath of a cold fog. Absurd, her reason told her, as she accepted Bellew's proffered light for her cigarette. Another glance at Clare showed her smiling. So, as one always ready to oblige, was Gertrude.

An on-looker, Irene reflected, would have thought it a most congenial tea-party, all smiles and jokes and hilarious laughter. She said humorously: "So you dislike Negroes, Mr. Bellew?" But her amusement was at her thought, rather than her words.

John Bellew gave a short denying laugh. "You got me wrong there, Mrs. Redfield. Nothing like that at all. I don't dislike them, I hate them. And so does Nig, for all she's trying to turn into one. She wouldn't have a nigger maid around her for love nor money. Not that I'd want her to. They give me the creeps. The black scrimy devils."

This wasn't funny. Had Bellew, Irene inquired, ever known any Negroes? The defensive tone of her voice brought another start from the uncomfortable Gertrude, and, for all her appearance of serenity, a quick apprehensive look from Clare.

Bellew answered: "Thank the Lord, no! And never expect to! But I know people who've known them, better than they know their black selves. And I read in the papers about them. Always robbing and killing people. And," he added darkly, "worse."

From Gertrude's direction came a queer little suppressed sound, a snort or a giggle. Irene couldn't tell which. There was a brief silence, during which she feared that her self control was about to prove too frail a bridge to support her mounting anger and indignation. She had a leaping desire to shout at the man beside her: "And you're sitting here surrounded by three black devils, drinking tea."

The impulse passed, obliterated by her consciousness of the danger in which such rashness would involve Clare, who remarked with a gentle reprovingness: "Jack dear, I'm sure 'Rene doesn't care to hear all about your pet aversions. Nor Gertrude either. Maybe they read the papers too, you know." She smiled on him, and her smile seemed to transform him, to soften and mellow him, as the rays of the sun does a fruit.

"All right, Nig, old girl. I'm sorry," he apologized. Reaching over, he playfully touched his wife's pale hands, then turned back to Irene. "Didn't mean to bore you, Mrs. Redfield. Hope you'll excuse me," he said sheepishly. "Clare tells me you're living in New York. Great city, New York. The city of the future."

In Irene, rage had not retreated, but was held by some dam of caution and allegiance to Clare. So, in the best casual voice she could muster, she agreed with

Bellew. Though, she reminded him, it was exactly what Chicagoans were apt to say of their city. And all the while she was speaking, she was thinking how amazing it was that her voice did not tremble, that outwardly she was calm. Only her hands shook slightly. She drew them inward from their rest in her lap and pressed the tips of her fingers together to still them.

"Husband's a doctor, I understand. Manhattan, or one of the other boroughs?"

Manhattan, Irene informed him, and explained the need for Brian to be within easy reach of certain hospitals and clinics.

"Interesting life, a doctor's."

"Ye-es. Hard, though. And, in a way, monotonous. Nerve-racking too."

"Hard on the wife's nerves at least, eh? So many lady patients." He laughed, enjoying, with a boyish heartiness, the hoary joke.

Irene managed a momentary smile, but her voice was sober as she said: "Brian doesn't care for ladies, especially sick ones. I sometimes wish he did. It's South America that attracts him."

"Coming place, South America, if they ever get the niggers out of it. It's run over—"

"Really, Jack!" Clare's voice was on the edge of temper.

"Honestly, Nig, I forgot." To the others he said: "You see how hen-pecked I am." And to Gertrude: "You're still in Chicago, Mrs.—er—Mrs. Martin?"

He was, it was plain, doing his best to be agreeable to these old friends of Clare's. Irene had to concede that under other conditions she might have liked him. A fairly good-looking man of amiable disposition, evidently, and in easy circumstances. Plain and with no nonsense about him.

Gertrude replied that Chicago was good enough for her. She'd never been out of it and didn't think she ever should. Her husband's business was there.

"Of course, of course. Can't jump up and leave a business."

There followed a smooth surface of talk about Chicago, New York, their differences and their recent spectacular changes.

It was, Irene, thought, unbelievable and astonishing that four people could sit so unruffled, so ostensibly friendly, while they were in reality seething with anger, mortification, shame. But no, on second thought she was forced to amend her opinion. John Bellew, most certainly, was as undisturbed within as without. So, perhaps, was Gertrude Martin. At least she hadn't the mortification and shame that Clare Kendry must be feeling, or, in such full measure, the rage and rebellion that she, Irene, was repressing.

"More tea, 'Rene," Clare offered.

"Thanks, no. And I must be going. I'm leaving tomorrow, you know, and I've still got packing to do."

She stood up. So did Gertrude, and Clare, and John Bellew.

"How do you like the Drayton, Mrs. Redfield?" the latter asked.

"The Drayton? Oh, very much. Very much indeed," Irene answered, her scornful eyes on Clare's unrevealing face.

"Nice place, all right. Stayed there a time or two myself," the man informed her.

"Yes, it is nice," Irene agreed. "Almost as good as our best New York places." She had withdrawn her look from Clare and was searching in her bag for some non-existent something. Her understanding was rapidly increasing, as was her pity and her contempt. Clare was so daring, so lovely, and so "having."

They gave their hands to Clare with appropriate murmurs. "So good to have seen you." . . . "I do hope I'll see you again soon."

"Good-bye," Clare returned. "It was good of you to come, 'Rene dear. And you too, Gertrude."

"Good-bye, Mr. Bellew." . . . "So glad to have met you." It was Gertrude who had said that. Irene couldn't, she absolutely couldn't bring herself to utter the polite fiction or anything approaching it.

He accompanied them out into the hall, summoned the elevator.

"Good-bye," they said again, stepping in.

Plunging downward they were silent.

They made their way through the lobby without speaking.

But as soon as they had reached the street Gertrude, in the manner of one unable to keep bottled up for another minute that which for the last hour she had had to retain, burst out: "My God! What an awful chance! She must be plumb crazy."

"Yes, it certainly seems risky," Irene admitted.

"Risky! I should say it was. Risky! My God! What a word! And the mess she's liable to get herself into!"

"Still, I imagine she's pretty safe. They don't live here, you know. And there's a child. That's a certain security."

"It's an awful chance, just the same," Gertrude insisted. "I'd never in the world have married Fred without him knowing. You can't tell what will turn up."

"Yes, I do agree that it's safer to tell. But then

Bellew wouldn't have married her. And, after all, that's what she wanted."

Gertrude shook her head. "I wouldn't be in her shoes for all the money she's getting out of it, when he finds out. Not with him feeling the way he does. Gee! Wasn't it awful? For a minute I was so mad I could have slapped him."

It had been, Irene acknowledged, a distinctly trying experience, as well as a very unpleasant one. "I was more than a little angry myself."

"And imagine her not telling us about him feeling that way! Anything might have happened. We might have said something."

That, Irene pointed out, was exactly like Clare Kendry. Taking a chance, and not at all considering anyone else's feelings.

Gertrude said: "Maybe she thought we'd think it a good joke. And I guess you did. The way you laughed. My land! I was scared to death he might catch on."

"Well, it was rather a joke," Irene told her, "on him and us and maybe on her."

"All the same, it's an awful chance. I'd hate to be her."

"She seems satisfied enough. She's got what she wanted, and the other day she told me it was worth it."

But about that Gertrude was sceptical. "She'll find

out different," was her verdict. "She'll find out different all right."

Rain had begun to fall, a few scattered large drops.

The end-of-the-day crowds were scurrying in the
directions of street-cars and elevated roads.

Irene said: "You're going south? I'm sorry. I've got
an errand. If you don't mind, I'll just say good-bye
here. It has been nice seeing you, Gertrude. Say hello
to Fred for me, and to your mother if she remembers
me. Good-bye."

She had wanted to be free of the other woman, to
be alone; for she was still sore and angry.

What right, she kept demanding of herself, had
Clare Kendry to expose her, or even Gertrude Martin, to such humiliation, such downright insult?

And all the while, on the rushing ride out to her father's house, Irene Redfield was trying to understand
the look on Clare's face as she had said good-bye.
Partly mocking, it had seemed, and partly menacing.
And something else for which she could find no
name.[4] For an instant a recrudescence of that sensation of fear which she had had while looking into
Clare's eyes that afternoon touched her. A slight
shiver ran over her.

"It's nothing," she told herself. "Just somebody
walking over my grave, as the children say." She tried

a tiny laugh and was annoyed to find that it was close to tears.

What a state she had allowed that horrible Bellew to get her into!

And late that night, even, long after the last guest had gone and the old house was quiet, she stood at her window frowning out into the dark rain and puzzling again over that look on Clare's incredibly beautiful face. She couldn't, however, come to any conclusion about its meaning, try as she might. It was unfathomable, utterly beyond any experience or comprehension of hers.

She turned away from the window, at last, with a still deeper frown. Why, after all, worry about Clare Kendry? She was well able to take care of herself, had always been able. And there were, for Irene, other things, more personal and more important to worry about.

Besides, her reason told her, she had only herself to blame for her disagreeable afternoon and its attendant fears and questions. She ought never to have gone.

FOUR

The next morning, the day of her departure for New York, had brought a letter, which, at first glance, she had instinctively known came from Clare Kendry, though she couldn't remember ever having had a letter from her before. Ripping it open and looking at the signature, she saw that she had been right in her guess. She wouldn't, she told herself, read it. She hadn't the time. And, besides, she had no wish to be reminded of the afternoon before. As it was, she felt none too fresh for her journey; she had had a wretched night. And all because of Clare's innate lack of consideration for the feelings of others.

But she did read it. After father and friends had waved good-bye, and she was being hurled eastward, she became possessed of an uncontrollable curiosity to see what Clare had said about yesterday. For what, she asked, as she took it out of her bag and opened it, could she, what could anyone, say about a thing like that?

Clare Kendry had said:

'Rene dear:

However am I to thank you for your visit? I know you are feeling that under the circumstances I ought not to have asked you to come, or, rather, insisted. But if you could know how glad, how excitingly happy, I was to meet you and how I ached to see more of you (to see everybody and couldn't), you would understand my wanting to see you again, and maybe forgive me a little.

My love to you always and always and to your dear father, and all my poor thanks.

Clare.

And there was a postscript which said:

It may be, 'Rene dear, it may just be, that, after all, your way may be the wiser and infinitely happier one. I'm not sure just now. At least not so sure as I have been.

C.

But the letter hadn't conciliated Irene. Her indignation was not lessened by Clare's flattering reference to her wiseness. As if, she thought wrathfully, anything could take away the humiliation, or any part of it, of what she had gone through yesterday afternoon for Clare Kendry.

With an unusual methodicalness she tore the offending letter into tiny ragged squares that fluttered down and made a small heap in her black *crêpe de Chine* lap. The destruction completed, she gathered them up, rose, and moved to the train's end. Standing there, she dropped them over the railing and watched them scatter, on tracks, on cinders, on forlorn grass, in rills of dirty water.

And that, she told herself, was that. The chances were one in a million that she would ever again lay eyes on Clare Kendry. If, however, that millionth chance should turn up, she had only to turn away her eyes, to refuse her recognition.

She dropped Clare out of her mind and turned her thoughts to her own affairs. To home, to the boys, to Brian. Brian, who in the morning would be waiting for her in the great clamourous station. She hoped that he had been comfortable and not too lonely without her and the boys. Not so lonely that that old, queer, unhappy restlessness had begun again within him, that craving for some place strange and different, which at the beginning of her marriage she had had to make such strenuous efforts to repress, and which yet faintly alarmed her, though it now sprang up at gradually lessening intervals.

PART TWO

RE-ENCOUNTER

ONE

Such were Irene Redfield's memories as she sat there in her room, a flood of October sunlight streaming in upon her, holding that second letter of Clare Kendry's.

Laying it aside, she regarded with an astonishment that had in it a mild degree of amusement the violence of the feelings which it stirred in her.

It wasn't the great measure of anger that surprised and slightly amused her. That, she was certain, was justified and reasonable, as was the fact that it could hold, still strong and unabated, across the stretch of two years' time entirely removed from any sight or sound of John Bellew, or of Clare. That even at this remote date the memory of the man's words and manner had power to set her hands to trembling and to send the blood pounding against her temples did not seem to her extraordinary. But that she should retain that dim sense of fear, of panic, was surprising, silly.

That Clare should have written, should even all things considered, have expressed a desire to see her again, did not so much amaze her. To count as nothing the annoyances, the bitterness, or the suffering of others, that was Clare.

Well—Irene's shoulders went up—one thing was sure: that she needn't, and didn't intend to, lay herself open to any repetition of a humiliation as galling and outrageous as that which, for Clare Kendry's sake, she had borne "that time in Chicago." Once was enough.

If, at the time of choosing, Clare hadn't precisely reckoned the cost, she had, nevertheless, no right to expect others to help make up the reckoning. The trouble with Clare was, not only that she wanted to have her cake and eat it too, but that she wanted to nibble at the cakes of other folk as well.

Irene Redfield found it hard to sympathize with this new tenderness, this avowed yearning of Clare's for "my own people."

The letter which she just put out of her hand was, to her taste, a bit too lavish in its wordiness, a shade too unreserved in the manner of its expression. It roused again that old suspicion that Clare was acting, not consciously, perhaps—that is, not too consciously—but, none the less, acting. Nor was Irene inclined to excuse what she termed Clare's downright selfishness.

And mingled with her disbelief and resentment was another feeling, a question. Why hadn't she spoken that day? Why, in the face of Bellew's ignorant hate and aversion, had she concealed her own origin? Why had she allowed him to make his assertions and express his misconceptions undisputed? Why, simply because of Clare Kendry, who had exposed her to such torment, had she failed to take up the defence of the race to which she belonged?

Irene asked these questions, felt them. They were, however, merely rhetorical, as she herself was well aware. She knew their answers, every one, and it was the same for them all. The sardony[1] of it! She couldn't betray Clare, couldn't even run the risk of appearing to defend a people that were being maligned, for fear that that defence might in some infinitesimal degree lead the way to final discovery of her secret. She had to Clare Kendry a duty. She was bound to her by those very ties of race, which, for all her repudiation of them, Clare had been unable to completely sever.

And it wasn't, as Irene knew, that Clare cared at all

about the race or what was to become of it. She didn't. Or that she had for any of its members great, or even real, affection, though she professed undying gratitude for the small kindnesses which the Westover family had shown her when she was a child. Irene doubted the genuineness of it, seeing herself only as a means to an end where Clare was concerned. Nor could it be said that she had even the slight artistic or sociological interest in the race that some members of other races displayed. She hadn't. No, Clare Kendry cared nothing for the race. She only belonged to it.

"Not another damned thing!" Irene declared aloud as she drew a fragile stocking over a pale beige-coloured foot.

"Aha! Swearing again, are you, madam? Caught you in the act that time."

Brian Redfield had come into the room in that noiseless way which, in spite, of the years of their life together, still had the power to disconcert her. He stood looking down on her with that amused smile of his, which was just the faintest bit supercilious and yet was somehow very becoming to him.

Hastily Irene pulled on the other stocking and slipped her feet into the slippers beside her chair.

"And what brought on this particular outburst of

profanity? That is, if an indulgent but perturbed husband may inquire. The mother of sons too! The times, alas, the times!"

"I've had this letter," Irene told him. "And I'm sure that anybody'll admit it's enough to make a saint swear. The nerve of her!"

She passed the letter to him, and in the act made a little mental frown. For, with a nicety of perception, she saw that she was doing it instead of answering his question with words, so that he might be occupied while she hurried through her dressing. For she was late again, and Brian, she well knew, detested that. Why, oh, why, couldn't she ever manage to be on time? Brian had been up for ages, had made some calls for all she knew, besides having taken the boys downtown to school. And she wasn't dressed yet; had only begun. Damn Clare! This morning it was her fault.

Brian sat down and bent his head over the letter, puckering his brows slightly in his effort to make out Clare's scrawl.

Irene, who had risen and was standing before the mirror, ran a comb through her black hair, then tossed her head with a light characteristic gesture, in order to disarrange a little the set locks. She touched a powder-puff to her warm olive skin, and then put on her frock with a motion so hasty that it was with some difficulty properly adjusted. At last she was ready, though she didn't immediately say so, but stood, instead, looking with a sort of curious detachment at her husband across the room.

Brian, she was thinking, was extremely good-looking. Not, of course, pretty or effeminate; the slight irregularity of his nose saved him from the prettiness, and the rather marked heaviness of his chin saved him from the effeminacy. But he was, in a pleasant masculine way, rather handsome. And yet, wouldn't he, perhaps, have been merely ordinarily good-looking but for the richness, the beauty of his skin, which was of an exquisitely fine texture and deep copper colour.

He looked up and said: "Clare? That must be the girl you told me about meeting the last time you were out home. The one you went to tea with?"

Irene's answer to that was an inclination of the head.

"I'm ready," she said.

They were going downstairs, Brian deftly, unnecessarily, piloting her round the two short curved steps, just before the centre landing.

"You're not," he asked, "going to see her?"

His words, however, were in reality not a question, but, as Irene was aware, an admonition.

Her front teeth just touched. She spoke through them, and her tones held a thin sarcasm. "Brian, darling, I'm really not such an idiot that I don't realize that if a man calls me a nigger, it's his fault the first time, but mine if he has the opportunity to do it again."

They went into the dining-room. He drew back her chair and she sat down behind the fat-bellied German coffee-pot, which sent out its morning fragrance, mingled with the smell of crisp toast and savoury bacon, in the distance. With his long, nervous fingers he picked up the morning paper from his own chair and sat down.

Zulena, a small mahogany-coloured creature, brought in the grapefruit.

They took up their spoons.

Out of the silence Brian spoke. Blandly. "My dear, you misunderstand me entirely. I simply meant that I hope you're not going to let her pester you. She will, you know, if you give her half a chance and she's anything at all like your description of her. Anyway, they always do. Besides," he corrected, "the man, her husband, didn't call you a nigger. There's a difference, you know."

"No, certainly he didn't. Not actually. He couldn't, not very well, since he didn't know. But he would have. It amounts to the same thing. And I'm sure it was just as unpleasant."

"U-mm, I don't know. But it seems to me," he pointed out, "that you, my dear, had all the advantage. You knew what his opinion of you was, while he— Well, 'twas ever thus. We know, always have. They don't. Not quite. It has, you will admit, its humorous side, and, sometimes, its conveniences."

She poured the coffee.

"I can't see it. I'm going to write Clare. Today, if I can find a minute. It's a thing we might as well settle definitely, and immediately. Curious, isn't it, that knowing, as she does, his unqualified attitude, she still—"

Brian interrupted: "It's always that way. Never known it to fail. Remember Albert Hammond, how he used to be for ever haunting Seventh Avenue, and Lenox Avenue,[2] and the dancing-places, until some 'shine'[3] took a shot at him for casting an eye towards his 'sheba?'[4] They always come back. I've seen it happen time and time again."

"But why?" Irene wanted to know. "Why?"

"If I knew that, I'd know what race is."

"But wouldn't you think that having got the thing,

or things, they were after, and at such risk, they'd be satisfied? Or afraid?"

"Yes," Brian agreed, "you certainly would think so. But, the fact remains, they aren't. Not satisfied, I mean. I think they're scared enough most of the time, when they give way to the urge and slip back. Not scared enough to stop them, though. Why, the good God only knows."

Irene leaned forward, speaking, she was aware, with a vehemence absolutely unnecessary, but which she could not control.

"Well, Clare can just count me out. I've no intention of being the link between her and her poorer darker brethren. After that scene in Chicago too! To calmly expect me—" She stopped short, suddenly too wrathful for words.

"Quite right. The only sensible thing to do. Let her miss you. It's an unhealthy business, the whole affair. Always is."

Irene nodded. "More coffee," she offered.

"Thanks, no." He took up his paper again, spreading it open with a little rattling noise.

Zulena came in bringing more toast. Brian took a slice and bit into it with that audible crunching sound that Irene disliked so intensely, and turned back to his paper.

She said: "It's funny about 'passing.' We disapprove of it and at the same time condone it. It excites our contempt and yet we rather admire it. We shy away from it with an odd kind of revulsion, but we protect it."

"Instinct of the race to survive and expand."[5]

"Rot! Everything can't be explained by some general biological phrase."

"Absolutely everything can. Look at the so-called whites, who've left bastards all over the known earth. Same thing in them. Instinct of the race to survive and expand."

With that Irene didn't at all agree, but many arguments in the past had taught her the futility of attempting to combat Brian on ground where he was more nearly at home than she. Ignoring his unqualified assertion, she slid away from the subject entirely.

"I wonder," she asked, "if you'll have time to run me down to the printing-office. It's on a Hundred and Sixteenth Street. I've got to see about some handbills and some more tickets for the dance."

"Yes, of course. How's it going? Everything all set?"

"Ye-es. I guess so. The boxes are all sold and nearly all the first batch of tickets. And we expect to take in almost as much again at the door. Then, there's all that cake to sell. It's a terrible lot of work, though."

"I'll bet it is. Uplifting the brother's no easy job. I'm as busy as a cat with fleas, myself." And over his face there came a shadow. "Lord! how I hate sick people, and their stupid, meddling families, and smelly, dirty rooms, and climbing filthy steps in dark hallways."

"Surely," Irene began, fighting back the fear and irritation that she felt, "surely—"

Her husband silenced her, saying sharply: "Let's not talk about it, please." And immediately, in his usual, slightly mocking tone he asked: "Are you ready to go now? I haven't a great deal of time to wait."

He got up. She followed him out into the hall without replying. He picked up his soft brown hat from the small table and stood a moment whirling it round on his long tea-coloured fingers.

Irene, watching him, was thinking: "It isn't fair, it isn't fair." After all these years to still blame her like this. Hadn't his success proved that she'd been right in insisting that he stick to his profession right there in New York? Couldn't he see, even now, that it *had* been best? Not for her, oh no, not for her—she had never really considered herself—but for him and the boys. Was she never to be free of it, that fear which crouched, always, deep down within her, stealing away the sense of security, the feeling of permanence, from the life which she had so admirably arranged for them all, and desired so ardently to have remain as it was? That strange, and to her fantastic, notion of Brian's of going off to Brazil, which, though unmentioned, yet lived within him; how it frightened her, and—yes, angered her!

"Well?" he asked lightly.

"I'll just get my things. One minute," she promised and turned upstairs.

Her voice had been even and her step was firm, but in her there was no slackening of the agitation, of the alarms, which Brian's expression of discontent had raised. He had never spoken of his desire since that long-ago time of storm and strain, of hateful and nearly disastrous quarrelling, when she had so firmly opposed him, so sensibly pointed out its utter impossibility and its probable consequences to her and the boys, and had even hinted at a dissolution of their marriage in the event of his persistence in his idea. No, there had been, in all the years that they had lived together since then, no other talk of it, no more than there had been any other quarrelling or any other threats. But because, so she insisted, the bond of flesh and spirit between them was so strong, she knew, had always known, that his dissatisfaction had continued, as had his dislike and disgust for his profession and his country.

A feeling of uneasiness stole upon her at the inconceivable suspicion that she might have been wrong in her estimate of her husband's character. But she squirmed away from it. Impossible! She couldn't have been wrong. Everything proved that she had been right. More than right, if such a thing could be. And all, she assured herself, because she understood him so well, because she had, actually, a special talent for understanding him. It was, as she saw it, the one thing that had been the basis of the success which she had made of a marriage that had threatened to fail. She knew him as well as he knew himself, or better.

Then why worry? The thing, this discontent which had exploded into words, would surely die, flicker out, at last. True, she had in the past often been tempted to believe that it had died, only to become conscious, in some instinctive, subtle way, that she had been merely deceiving herself for a while and that it still lived. But it *would* die. Of that she was certain. She had only to direct and guide her man, to keep him going in the right direction.

She put on her coat and adjusted her hat.

Yes, it would die, as long ago she had made up her mind that it should. But in the meantime, while it was still living and still had the power to flare up and alarm her, it would have to be banked, smothered, and something offered in its stead. She would have to make some plan, some decision, at once. She frowned, for it annoyed her intensely. For, though temporary, it would be important and perhaps disturbing. Irene didn't like changes, particularly changes that affected the smooth routine of her household. Well, it couldn't be helped. Something would have to be done. And immediately.

She took up her purse and drawing on her gloves, ran down the steps and out through the door which Brian held open for her and stepped into the waiting car.

"You know," she said, settling herself into the seat beside him, "I'm awfully glad to get this minute alone with you. It does seem that we're always so busy—I do hate that—but what can we do? I've had something on my mind for ever so long, something that needs talking over and really serious consideration."

The car's engine rumbled as it moved out from the kerb and into the scant traffic of the street under Brian's expert guidance.

She studied his profile.

They turned into Seventh Avenue. Then he said: "Well, let's have it. No time like the present for the settling of weighty matters."

"It's about Junior. I wonder if he isn't going too fast

in school? We do forget that he's not eleven yet. Surely it can't be good for him to—well, if he is, I mean. Going too fast, you know. Of course, you know more about these things than I do. You're better able to judge. That is, if you've noticed or thought about it at all."

"I do wish, Irene, you wouldn't be for ever fretting about those kids. They're all right. Perfectly all right. Good, strong, healthy boys, especially Junior. Most especially Junior."

"We-ll, I s'pose you're right. You're expected to know about things like that, and I'm sure you wouldn't make a mistake about your own boy." (Now, why had she said that?) "But that isn't all. I'm terribly afraid he's picked up some queer ideas about things— some things—from the older boys, you know."

Her manner was consciously light. Apparently she was intent on the maze of traffic, but she was still watching Brian's face closely. On it was a peculiar expression. Was it, could it possibly be, a mixture of scorn and distaste?

"Queer ideas?" he repeated. "D'you mean ideas about sex, Irene?"

"Ye-es. Not quite nice ones. Dreadful jokes, and things like that."

"Oh, I see," he threw at her. For a while there was

silence between them. After a moment he demanded bluntly: "Well, what of it? If sex isn't a joke, what is it? And what is a joke?"

"As you please, Brian. He's your son, you know." Her voice was clear, level, disapproving.

"Exactly! And you're trying to make a molly-coddle out of him. Well, just let me tell you, I won't have it. And you needn't think I'm going to let you change him to some nice kindergarten kind of a school because he's getting a little necessary education. I won't! He'll stay right where he is. The sooner and the more he learns about sex, the better for him. And most certainly if he learns that it's a grand joke, the greatest in the world. It'll keep him from lots of disappointments later on."

Irene didn't answer.

They reached the printing-shop. She got out, emphatically slamming the car's door behind her. There was a piercing agony of misery in her heart. She hadn't intended to behave like this, but her extreme resentment at his attitude, the sense of having been wilfully misunderstood and reproved, drove her to fury.

Inside the shop, she stilled the trembling of her lips and drove back her rising anger. Her business transacted, she came back to the car in a chastened mood.

But against the armour of Brian's stubborn silence she heard herself saying in a calm, metallic voice: "I don't believe I'll go back just now. I've remembered that I've got to do something about getting something decent to wear. I haven't a rag that's fit to be seen. I'll take the bus downtown."

Brian merely doffed his hat in that maddening polite way which so successfully curbed and yet revealed his temper.

"Good-bye," she said bitingly. "Thanks for the lift," and turned towards the avenue.

What, she wondered contritely, was she to do next? She was vexed with herself for having chosen, as it had turned out, so clumsy an opening for what she had intended to suggest: some European school for Junior next year, and Brian to take him over. If she had been able to present her plan, and he had accepted it, as she was sure that he would have done, with other more favourable opening methods, he would have had that to look forward to as a break in the easy monotony that seemed, for some reason she was wholly unable to grasp, so hateful to him.

She was even more vexed at her own explosion of anger. What could have got into her to give way to it in such a moment?

Gradually her mood passed. She drew back from

the failure of her first attempt at substitution, not so much discouraged as disappointed and ashamed. It might be, she reflected, that, in addition to her ill-timed loss of temper, she had been too hasty in her eagerness to distract him, had rushed too closely on the heels of his outburst, and had thus aroused his suspicions and his obstinacy. She had but to wait. Another more appropriate time would come, tomorrow, next week, next month. It wasn't now, as it had been once, that she was afraid that he would throw everything aside and rush off to that remote place of his heart's desire. He wouldn't, she knew. He was fond of her, loved her, in his slightly undemonstrative way.

And there were the boys.

It was only that she wanted him to be happy, resenting, however, his inability to be so with things as they were, and never acknowledging that though she did want him to be happy, it was only in her own way and by some plan of hers for him that she truly desired him to be so. Nor did she admit that all other plans, all other ways, she regarded as menaces, more or less indirect, to that security of place and substance which she insisted upon for her sons and in a lesser degree for herself.

TWO

Five days had gone by since Clare Kendry's appealing letter. Irene Redfield had not replied to it. Nor had she had any other word from Clare.

She had not carried out her first intention of writing at once because on going back to the letter for Clare's address, she had come upon something which, in the rigour of her determination to maintain unbroken between them the wall that Clare herself had raised, she had forgotten, or not fully noted. It was the fact that Clare had requested her to direct her answer to the post office's general delivery.

That had angered Irene, and increased her disdain and contempt for the other.

Tearing the letter across, she had flung it into the scrapbasket. It wasn't so much Clare's carefulness and her desire for secrecy in their relations—Irene understood the need for that—as that Clare should have doubted her discretion, implied that she might not be cautious in the wording of her reply and the choice of a posting-box. Having always had complete confidence in her own good judgment and tact, Irene couldn't bear to have anyone seem to question them. Certainly not Clare Kendry.

In another, calmer moment she decided that it was, after all, better to answer nothing, to explain nothing, to refuse nothing; to dispose of the matter simply by not writing at all. Clare, of whom it couldn't be said that she was stupid, would not mistake the implication of that silence. She might—and Irene was sure that she would—choose to ignore it and write again, but that didn't matter. The whole thing would be very easy. The basket for all letters, silence for their answers.

Most likely she and Clare would never meet again. Well, she, for one, could endure that. Since childhood their lives had never really touched. Actually they were strangers. Strangers in their ways and means of living. Strangers in their desires and ambitions.

Strangers even in their racial consciousness. Between them the barrier was just as high, just as broad, and just as firm as if in Clare did not run that strain of black blood. In truth, it was higher, broader, and firmer; because for her there were perils, not known, or imagined, by those others who had no such secrets to alarm or endanger them.

———

The day was getting on toward evening. It was past the middle of October. There had been a week of cold rain, drenching the rotting leaves which had fallen from the poor trees that lined the street on which the Redfields' house was located, and sending a damp air of penetrating chill into the house, with a hint of cold days to come. In Irene's room a low fire was burning. Outside, only a dull grey light was left of the day. Inside, lamps had already been lighted.

From the floor above there was the sound of young voices. Sometimes Junior's serious and positive; again, Ted's deceptively gracious one. Often there was laughter, or the noise of commotion, tussling, or toys being slammed down.

Junior, tall for his age, was almost incredibly like his father in feature and colouring; but his temperament was hers, practical and determined, rather than

Brian's. Ted, speculative and withdrawn, was, apparently, less positive in his ideas and desires. About him there was a deceiving air of candour that was, Irene knew, like his father's show of reasonable acquiescence. If, for the time being, and with a charming appearance of artlessness, he submitted to the force of superior strength, or some other immovable condition or circumstance, it was because of his intense dislike of scenes and unpleasant argument. Brian over again.

Gradually Irene's thought slipped away from Junior and Ted, to become wholly absorbed in their father.

The old fear, with strength increased, the fear for the future, had again laid its hand on her. And, try as she might, she could not shake it off. It was as if she had admitted to herself that against that easy surface of her husband's concordance with her wishes, which had, since the war had given him back to her physically unimpaired, covered an increasing inclination to tear himself and his possessions loose from their proper setting, she was helpless.

The chagrin which she had felt at her first failure to subvert this latest manifestation of his discontent had receded, leaving in its wake an uneasy depression. Were all her efforts, all her labours, to make up to him that one loss, all her silent striving to prove to him that her way had been best, all her ministrations to him, all her outward sinking of self, to count for nothing in some unperceived sudden moment? And if so, what, then, would be the consequences to the boys? To her? To Brian himself? Endless searching had brought no answer to these questions. There was only an intense weariness from their shuttle-like procession in her brain.

The noise and commotion from above grew increasingly louder. Irene was about to go to the stairway and request the boys to be quieter in their play when she heard the doorbell ringing.

Now, who was that likely to be? She listened to Zulena's heels, faintly tapping on their way to the door, then to the shifting sound of her feet on the steps, then to her light knock on the bedroom door.

"Yes. Come in," Irene told her.

Zulena stood in the doorway. She said: "Someone to see you, Mrs. Redfield." Her tone was discreetly regretful, as if to convey that she was reluctant to disturb her mistress at that hour, and for a stranger. "A Mrs. Bellew."

Clare!

"Oh dear! Tell her, Zulena," Irene began, "that I can't—No. I'll see her. Please bring her up here."

She heard Zulena pass down the hall, down the stairs, then stood up, smoothing out the tumbled green and ivory draperies of her dress with light stroking pats. At the mirror she dusted a little powder on her nose and brushed out her hair.

She meant to tell Clare Kendry at once, and definitely, that it was of no use, her coming, that she couldn't be responsible, that she'd talked it over with Brian, who had agreed with her that it was wiser, for Clare's own sake, to refrain—

But that was as far as she got in her rehearsal. For Clare had come softly into the room without knocking, and before Irene could greet her, had dropped a kiss on her dark curls.

Looking at the woman before her, Irene Redfield had a sudden inexplicable onrush of affectionate feeling. Reaching out, she grasped Clare's two hands in her own and cried with something like awe in her voice: "Dear God! But aren't you lovely, Clare!"

Clare tossed that aside. Like the furs and small blue hat which she threw on the bed before seating herself slantwise in Irene's favourite chair, with one foot curled under her.

"Didn't you mean to answer my letter, 'Rene?" she asked gravely.

Irene looked away. She had that uncomfortable

feeling that one has when one has not been wholly kind or wholly true.

Clare went on: "Every day I went to that nasty little post-office place. I'm sure they were all beginning to think that I'd been carrying on an illicit love-affair and that the man had thrown me over. Every morning the same answer: 'Nothing for you.' I got into an awful fright, thinking that something might have happened to your letter, or to mine. And half the nights I would lie awake looking out at the watery stars—hopeless things, the stars—worrying and wondering. But at last it soaked in, that you hadn't written and didn't intend to. And then—well, as soon as ever I'd seen Jack off for Florida, I came straight here. And now, 'Rene, please tell me quite frankly why you didn't answer my letter."

"Because, you see—" Irene broke off and kept Clare waiting while she lit a cigarette, blew out the match, and dropped it into a tray. She was trying to collect her arguments, for some sixth sense warned her that it was going to be harder than she thought to convince Clare Kendry of the folly of Harlem for her. Finally she proceeded: "I can't help thinking that you ought not to come up here, ought not to run the risk of knowing Negroes."

"You mean you don't want me, 'Rene?"

Irene hadn't supposed that anyone could look so hurt. She said, quite gently, "No, Clare, it's not that. But even you must see that it's terribly foolish, and not just the right thing."

The tinkle of Clare's laugh rang out, while she passed her hands over the bright sweep of her hair. "Oh, 'Rene!" she cried, "you're priceless! And you haven't changed a bit. The right thing!" Leaning forward, she looked curiously into Irene's disapproving brown eyes. "You don't, you really can't mean exactly that! Nobody could. It's simply unbelievable."

Irene was on her feet before she realized that she had risen. "What I really mean," she retorted, "is that it's dangerous and that you ought not to run such silly risks. No one ought to. You least of all."

Her voice was brittle. For into her mind had come a thought, strange and irrelevant, a suspicion, that had surprised and shocked her and driven her to her feet. It was that in spite of her determined selfishness the woman before her was yet capable of heights and depths of feeling that she, Irene Redfield, had never known. Indeed, never cared to know. The thought, the suspicion, was gone as quickly as it had come.

Clare said: "Oh, me!"

Irene touched her arm caressingly, as if in contrition for that flashing thought. "Yes, Clare, you. It's not safe. Not safe at all."

"Safe!"

It seemed to Irene that Clare had snapped her teeth down on the word and then flung it from her. And for another flying second she had that suspicion of Clare's ability for a quality of feeling that was to her strange, and even repugnant. She was aware, too, of a dim premonition of some impending disaster. It was as if Clare Kendry had said to her, for whom safety, security, were all-important: "Safe! Damn being safe!" and meant it.

With a gesture of impatience she sat down. In a voice of cool formality, she said: "Brian and I have talked the whole thing over carefully and decided that it isn't wise. He says it's always a dangerous business, this coming back. He's seen more than one come to grief because of it. And, Clare, considering everything—Mr. Bellew's attitude and all that—don't you think you ought to be as careful as you can?"

Clare's deep voice broke the small silence that had followed Irene's speech. She said, speaking almost plaintively: "I ought to have known. It's Jack. I don't blame you for being angry, though I must say you behaved beautifully that day. But I did think you'd understand, 'Rene. It was that, partly, that has made me want to see other people. It just swooped down and changed everything. If it hadn't been for that, I'd have gone on to the end, never seeing any of you. But that did something to me, and I've been so lonely since! You can't know. Not close to a single soul. Never anyone to really talk to."

Irene pressed out her cigarette. While doing so, she saw again the vision of Clare Kendry staring disdainfully down at the face of her father, and thought that it would be like that that she would look at her husband if he lay dead before her.

Her own resentment was swept aside and her voice held an accent of pity as she exclaimed: "Why, Clare! I didn't know. Forgive me. I feel like seven beasts. It was stupid of me not to realize."

"No. Not at all. You couldn't. Nobody, none of you, could," Clare moaned. The black eyes filled with tears that ran down her cheeks and spilled into her lap, ruining the priceless velvet of her dress. Her long hands were a little uplifted and clasped tightly together. Her effort to speak moderately was obvious, but not successful. "How could you know? How could you? You're free. You're happy. And," with faint derision, "safe."

Irene passed over that touch of derision, for the

poignant rebellion of the other's words had brought the tears to her own eyes, though she didn't allow them to fall. The truth was that she knew weeping did not become her. Few women, she imagined, wept as attractively as Clare. "I'm beginning to believe," she murmured, "that no one is ever completely happy, or free, or safe."

"Well, then, what does it matter? One risk more or less, if we're not safe anyway, if even you're not, it can't make all the difference in the world. It can't to me. Besides, I'm used to risks. And this isn't such a big one as you're trying to make it."

"Oh, but it is. And it can make all the difference in the world. There's your little girl, Clare. Think of the consequences to her."

Clare's face took on a startled look, as though she were totally unprepared for this new weapon with which Irene had assailed her. Seconds passed, during which she sat with stricken eyes and compressed lips. "I think," she said at last, "that being a mother is the cruellest thing in the world." Her clasped hands swayed forward and back again, and her scarlet mouth trembled irrepressibly.

"Yes," Irene softly agreed. For a moment she was unable to say more, so accurately had Clare put into words that which, not so definitely defined, was so often in her own heart of late. At the same time she was conscious that here, to her hand, was a reason which could not be lightly brushed aside. "Yes," she repeated, "and the most responsible, Clare. We mothers are all responsible for the security and happiness of our children. Think what it would mean to your Margery if Mr. Bellew should find out. You'd probably lose her. And even if you didn't, nothing that concerned her would ever be the same again. He'd never forget that she had Negro blood. And if she should learn—Well, I believe that after twelve it is too late to learn a thing like that. She'd never forgive you. You may be used to risks, but this is one you mustn't take, Clare. It's a selfish whim, an unnecessary and—

"Yes, Zulena, what is it?" she inquired, a trifle tartly, of the servant who had silently materialized in the doorway.

"The telephone's for you, Mrs. Redfield. It's Mr. Wentworth."[1]

"All right. Thank you. I'll take it here." And, with a muttered apology to Clare, she took up the instrument.

"Hello.... Yes, Hugh.... Oh, quite.... And you?... I'm sorry, every single thing's gone. . . . Oh, too bad. . . . Ye-es, I s'pose you could. Not very pleasant, though.... Yes, of course, in a pinch everything goes....

Wait! I've got it! I'll change mine with whoever's next to you, and you can have that. . . . No. . . . I mean it. . . . I'll be so busy I shan't know whether I'm sitting or standing. . . . As long as Brian has a place to drop down now and then. . . . Not a single soul. . . . No, don't. . . . That's nice. . . . My love to Bianca. . . . I'll see to it right away and call you back. . . . Good-bye."

She hung up and turned back to Clare, a little frown on her softly chiselled features. "It's the N. W. L. dance," she explained, "the Negro Welfare League,[2] you know. I'm on the ticket committee, or, rather, I *am* the committee. Thank heaven it comes off tomorrow night and doesn't happen again for a year. I'm about crazy, and now I've got to persuade somebody to change boxes with me."

"That wasn't," Clare asked, "Hugh Wentworth? Not *the* Hugh Wentworth?"

Irene inclined her head. On her face was a tiny triumphant smile. "Yes, *the* Hugh Wentworth. D'you know him?"

"No. How should I? But I do know about him. And I've read a book or two of his."

"Awfully good, aren't they?"

"U-umm, I s'pose so. Sort of contemptuous, I thought. As if he more or less despised everything and everybody."

"I shouldn't be a bit surprised if he did. Still, he's about earned the right to. Lived on the edges of nowhere in at least three continents. Been through every danger in all kinds of savage places. It's no wonder he thinks the rest of us are a lazy self-pampering lot. Hugh's a dear, though, generous as one of the twelve disciples; give you the shirt off his back. Bianca—that's his wife—is nice too."

"And he's coming up here to your dance?"

Irene asked why not.

"It seems rather curious, a man like that, going to a Negro dance."

This, Irene told her, was the year 1927 in the city of New York, and hundreds of white people of Hugh Wentworth's type came to affairs in Harlem, more all the time. So many that Brian had said: "Pretty soon the coloured people won't be allowed in at all, or will have to sit in Jim Crowed sections."

"What do they come for?"

"Same reason you're here, to see Negroes."

"But why?"

"Various motives," Irene explained. "A few purely and frankly to enjoy themselves. Others to get material to turn into shekels.³ More, to gaze on these great and near great while they gaze on the Negroes."

Clare clapped her hands. " 'Rene, suppose I come too! It sounds terribly interesting and amusing. And I don't see why I shouldn't."

Irene, who was regarding her through narrowed eyelids, had the same thought that she had had two years ago on the roof of the Drayton, that Clare Kendry was just a shade too good-looking. Her tone was on the edge of irony as she said: "You mean because so many other white people go?"

A pale rose-colour came into Clare's ivory cheeks. She lifted a hand in protest. "Don't be silly! Certainly not! I mean that in a crowd of that kind I shouldn't be noticed."

On the contrary, was Irene's opinion. It might be even doubly dangerous. Some friend or acquaintance of John Bellew or herself might see and recognize her.

At that, Clare laughed for a long time, little musical trills following one another in sequence after sequence. It was as if the thought of any friend of John Bellew's going to a Negro dance was to her the most amusing thing in the world.

"I don't think," she said, when she had done laughing, "we need worry about that."

Irene, however, wasn't so sure. But all her efforts to

dissuade Clare were useless. To her, "You never can tell whom you're likely to meet there," Clare's rejoinder was: "I'll take my chance on getting by."

"Besides, you won't know a soul and I shall be too busy to look after you. You'll be bored stiff."

"I won't, I won't. If nobody asks me to dance, not even Dr. Redfield, I'll just sit and gaze on the great and the near great, too. Do, 'Rene, be polite and invite me."

Irene turned away from the caress of Clare's smile, saying promptly and positively: "I will not."

"I mean to go anyway," Clare retorted, and her voice was no less positive than Irene's.

"Oh, no. You couldn't possibly go there alone. It's a public thing. All sorts of people go, anybody who can pay a dollar, even ladies of easy virtue looking for trade. If you were to go there alone, you might be mistaken for one of them, and that wouldn't be too pleasant."

Clare laughed again. "Thanks. I never have been. It might be amusing. I'm warning you, 'Rene, that if you're not going to be nice and take me, I'll still be among those present. I suppose, my dollar's as good as anyone's."

"Oh, the dollar! Don't be a fool, Claire. I don't care where you go, or what you do. All I'm concerned with is the unpleasantness and possible danger which your going might incur, because of your situation. To put it frankly, I shouldn't like to be mixed up in any row of the kind." She had risen again as she spoke and was standing at the window lifting and spreading the small yellow chrysanthemums in the grey stone jar on the sill. Her hands shook slightly, for she was in a near rage of impatience and exasperation.

Claire's face looked strange, as if she wanted to cry again. One of her satin-covered feet swung restlessly back and forth. She said vehemently, violently almost: "Damn Jack! He keeps me out of everything. Everything I want. I could kill him! I expect I shall, some day."

"I wouldn't," Irene advised her, "you see, there's still capital punishment, in this state at least. And really, Clare, after everything's said, I can't see that you've a right to put all the blame on him. You've got to admit that there's his side to the thing. You didn't tell him you were coloured, so he's got no way of knowing about this hankering of yours after Negroes, or that it galls you to fury to hear them called niggers and black devils. As far as I can see, you'll just have to endure some things and give up others. As we've said before, everything must be paid for. Do, please, be reasonable."

But Clare, it was plain, had shut away reason as well as caution. She shook her head. "I can't, I can't," she said. "I would if I could, but I can't. You don't know, you can't realize how I want to see Negroes, to be with them again, to talk with them, to hear them laugh."

And in the look she gave Irene, there was something groping, and hopeless, and yet so absolutely determined that it was like an image of the futile searching and the firm resolution in Irene's own soul, and increased the feeling of doubt and compunction that had been growing within her about Clare Kendry.

She gave in.

"Oh, come if you want to. I s'pose you're right. Once can't do such a terrible lot of harm."

Pushing aside Clare's extravagant thanks, for immediately she was sorry that she had consented, she said briskly: "Should you like to come up and see my boys?"

"I'd love to."

They went up, Irene thinking that Brian would consider that she'd behaved like a spineless fool. And he would be right. She certainly had.

Clare was smiling. She stood in the doorway of the

boys' playroom, her shadowy eyes looking down on Junior and Ted, who had sprung apart from their tusselling. Junior's face had a funny little look of resentment. Ted's was blank.

Clare said: "Please don't be cross. Of course, I know I've gone and spoiled everything. But maybe, if I promise not to get too much in the way, you'll let me come in, just the same."

"Sure, come in if you want to," Ted told her. "We can't stop you, you know." He smiled and made her a little bow and then turned away to a shelf that held his favourite books. Taking one down, he settled himself in a chair and began to read.

Junior said nothing, did nothing, merely stood there waiting.

"Get up, Ted! That's rude. This is Theodore, Mrs. Bellew. Please excuse his bad manners. He does know better. And this is Brian junior. Mrs. Bellew is an old friend of mother's. We used to play together when we were little girls."

———

Clare had gone and Brian had telephoned that he'd been detained and would have his dinner downtown. Irene was a little glad for that. She was going out later herself, and that meant she wouldn't, probably, see

Brian until morning and so could put off for a few
more hours speaking of Clare and the N. W. L. dance.

She was angry with herself and with Clare. But
more with herself, for having permitted Clare to
tease her into doing something that Brian had, all but
expressly, asked her not to do. She didn't want him
ruffled, not just then, not while he was possessed of
that unreasonable restless feeling.

She was annoyed, too, because she was aware that
she had consented to something which, if it went beyond the dance, would involve her in numerous petty
inconveniences and evasions. And not only at home
with Brian, but outside with friends and acquaintances. The disagreeable possibilities in connection
with Clare Kendry's coming among them loomed before her in endless irritating array.

Clare, it seemed, still retained her ability to secure
the thing that she wanted in the face of any opposition, and in utter disregard of the convenience and
desire of others. About her there was some quality,
hard and persistent, with the strength and endurance
of rock, that would not be beaten or ignored. She
couldn't, Irene thought, have had an entirely serene
life. Not with that dark secret for ever crouching in
the background of her consciousness. And yet she
hadn't the air of a woman whose life had been

touched by uncertainty or suffering. Pain, fear, and grief were things that left their mark on people. Even love, that exquisite torturing emotion, left its subtle traces on the countenance.

But Clare—she had remained almost what she had always been, an attractive, somewhat lonely child—selfish, wilful, and disturbing.

THREE

The things which Irene Redfield remembered afterward about the Negro Welfare League dance seemed, to her, unimportant and unrelated.

She remembered the not quite derisive smile with which Brian had cloaked his vexation when she informed him—oh, so apologetically—that she had promised to take Clare, and related the conversation of her visit.

She remembered her own little choked exclamation of admiration, when, on coming downstairs a few minutes later than she had intended, she had rushed into the living-room where Brian was waiting and had found Clare there too. Clare, exquisite, golden, fragrant, flaunting, in a stately gown of shining black taffeta, whose long, full skirt lay in graceful folds about her slim golden feet; her glistening hair drawn smoothly back into a small twist at the nape of her neck; her eyes sparkling like dark jewels. Irene, with her new rose-colored chiffon frock ending at the knees, and her cropped curls, felt dowdy and commonplace. She regretted that she hadn't counselled Clare to wear something ordinary and inconspicuous. What on earth would Brian think of deliberate courting of attention? But if Clare Kendry's appearance had in it anything that was, to Brian Redfield, annoying or displeasing, the fact was not discernible to his wife as, with an uneasy feeling of guilt, she stood there looking into his face while Clare explained that she and he had made their own introductions, accompanying her words with a little deferential smile for Brian, and receiving in return one of his amused, slightly mocking smiles.

She remembered Clare's saying, as they sped northward: "You know, I feel exactly as I used to on the Sunday we went to the Christmas-tree celebration. I knew there was to be a surprise for me and couldn't quite guess what it was to be. I am *so* excited. You can't possibly imagine! It's marvellous to be really on the way! I can hardly believe it!"

At her words and tone a chilly wave of scorn had crept through Irene. All those superlatives! She said, taking care to speak indifferently: "Well, maybe in some ways you will be surprised, more, probably, than you anticipate."

Brian, at the wheel, had thrown back: "And then again, she won't be so very surprised after all, for it'll no doubt be about what she expects. Like the Christmas-tree."

She remembered rushing around here and there, consulting with this person and that one, and now and then snatching a part of a dance with some man whose dancing she particularly liked.

She remembered catching glimpses of Clare in the whirling crowd, dancing, sometimes with a white man, more often with a Negro, frequently with Brian. Irene was glad that he was being nice to Clare, and glad that Clare was having the opportunity to discover that some coloured men were superior to some white men.

She remembered a conversation she had with Hugh Wentworth in a free half-hour when she had dropped into a chair in an emptied box and let her gaze wander over the bright crowd below.

Young men, old men, white men, black men; youthful women, older women, pink women, golden

women; fat men, thin men, tall men, short men; stout
women, slim women, stately women, small women
moved by. An old nursery rhyme popped into her
head. She turned to Wentworth, who had just taken a
seat beside her, and recited it:

> *"Rich man, poor man,*
> *Beggar man, thief,*
> *Doctor, lawyer,*
> *Indian chief."*[1]

"Yes," Wentworth said, "that's it. Everybody seems to
be here and a few more. But what I'm trying to find
out is the name, status, and race of the blonde beauty
out of the fairy-tale. She's dancing with Ralph Hazelton at the moment. Nice study in contrasts, that."

It was. Clare fair and golden, like a sunlit day.
Hazelton dark, with gleaming eyes, like a moonlit
night.

"She's a girl I used to know a long time ago in
Chicago. And she wanted especially to meet you."

" 'S awfully good of her, I'm sure. And now, alas!
the usual thing's happened. All these others, these—
er—'gentlemen of colour' have driven a mere Nordic[2]
from her mind."

"Stuff!"

" 'S a fact, and what happens to all the ladies of my superior race who're lured up here. Look at Bianca. Have I laid eyes on her tonight except in spots, here and there, being twirled about by some Ethiopian? I have not."

"But, Hugh, you've got to admit that the average coloured man is a better dancer than the average white man—that is, if the celebrities and 'butter and egg' men[3] who find their way up here are fair specimens of white Terpsichorean art."[4]

"Not having tripped the light fantastic with any of the males, I'm not in a position to argue the point. But I don't think it's merely that. 'S something else, some other attraction. They're always raving about the good looks of some Negro, preferably an unusually dark one. Take Hazelton there, for example. Dozens of women have declared him to be fascinatingly handsome. How about you, Irene? Do you think he's—er—ravishingly beautiful?"

"I do not! And I don't think the others do either. Not honestly, I mean. I think that what they feel is—well, a kind of emotional excitement. You know, the sort of thing you feel in the presence of something strange, and even, perhaps, a bit repugnant to you; something so different that it's really at the opposite end of the pole from all your accustomed notions of beauty."

"Damned if I don't think you're halfway right!"

"I'm sure I am. Completely. (Except, of course, when it's just patronizing kindness on their part.) And I know coloured girls who've experienced the same thing—the other way round, naturally."

"And the men? You don't subscribe to the general opinion about their reason for coming up here. Purely predatory. Or, do you?"

"N-no. More curious, I should say."

Wentworth, whose eyes were a clouded amber colour, had given her a long, searching look that was really a stare. He said: "All this is awfully interestin', Irene. We've got to have a long talk about it some time soon. There's your friend from Chicago, first time up here and all that. A case in point."

Irene's smile had only just lifted the corners of her painted lips. A match blazed in Wentworth's broad hands as he lighted her cigarette and his own, and flickered out before he asked: "Or isn't she?"

Her smile changed to a laugh. "Oh, Hugh! You're so clever. You usually know everything. Even how to tell the sheep from the goats. What do you think? Is she?"

He blew a long contemplative wreath of smoke.

"Damned if I know! I'll be as sure as anything that I've learned the trick. And then in the next minute I'll find I couldn't pick some of 'em if my life depended on it."

"Well, don't let that worry you. Nobody can. Not by looking."

"Not by looking, eh? Meaning?"

"I'm afraid I can't explain. Not clearly. There are ways. But they're not definite or tangible."

"Feeling of kinship, or something like that?"

"Good heavens, no! Nobody has that, except for their in-laws."

"Right again! But go on about the sheep and the goats."

"Well, take my own experience with Dorothy Thompkins. I'd met her four or five times, in groups and crowds of people, before I knew she wasn't a Negro. One day I went to an awful tea, terribly dicty.[5] Dorothy was there. We got talking. In less than five minutes, I knew she was 'fay.'[6] Not from anything she did or said or anything in her appearance. Just—just something. A thing that couldn't be registered."

"Yes, I understand what you mean. Yet lots of people 'pass' all the time."

"Not on our side, Hugh. It's easy for a Negro to 'pass' for white. But I don't think it would be so simple for a white person to 'pass' for coloured."

"Never thought of that."

"No, you wouldn't. Why should you?"

He regarded her critically through mists of smoke. "Slippin' me, Irene?"[7]

She said soberly: "Not you, Hugh. I'm too fond of you. And you're too sincere."

And she remembered that towards the end of the dance Brian had come to her and said: "I'll drop you first and then run Clare down." And that he had been doubtful of her discretion when she had explained to him that he wouldn't have to bother because she had asked Bianca Wentworth to take her down with them. Did she, he had asked, think it had been wise to tell them about Clare?

"I told them nothing," she said sharply, for she was unbearably tired, "except that she was at the Walsingham. It's on their way. And, really, I haven't thought anything about the wisdom of it, but now that I do, I'd say it's much better for them to take her than you."

"As you please. She's your friend, you know," he had answered, with a disclaiming shrug of his shoulders.

Except for these few unconnected things the dance faded to a blurred memory, its outlines mingling with those of other dances of its kind that she had attended in the past and would attend in the future.

FOUR

But undistinctive as the dance had seemed, it was, nevertheless, important. For it marked the beginning of a new factor in Irene Redfield's life, something that left its trace on all the future years of her existence. It was the beginning of a new friendship with Clare Kendry.

She came to them frequently after that. Always with a touching gladness that welled up and over-flowed on all the Redfield household. Yet Irene could never be sure whether her comings were a joy or a vexation.

Certainly she was no trouble. She had not to be en-tertained, or even noticed—if anyone could ever avoid noticing Clare. If Irene happened to be out or occupied, Clare could very happily amuse herself with Ted and Junior, who had conceived for her an admiration that verged on adoration, especially Ted. Or, lacking the boys, she would descend to the kitchen and, with—to Irene—an exasperating child-like lack of perception, spend her visit in talk and merriment with Zulena and Sadie.

Irene, while secretly resenting these visits to the playroom and kitchen, for some obscure reason which she shied away from putting into words, never requested that Clare make an end of them, or hinted that she wouldn't have spoiled her own Margery so outrageously, nor been so friendly with white servants.

Brian looked on these things with the same tolerant amusement that marked his entire attitude toward Clare. Never since his faintly derisive surprise at Irene's information that she was to go with them the night of the dance, had he shown any disapproval of Clare's presence. On the other hand, it couldn't be said that her presence seemed to please him. It didn't annoy or disturb him, so far as Irene could judge. That was all.

Didn't he, she once asked him, think Clare was extraordinarily beautiful?

"No," he had answered. "That is, not particularly."

"Brian, you're fooling!"

"No, honestly. Maybe I'm fussy. I s'pose she'd be an unusually good-looking white woman. I like my ladies darker. Beside an A-number-one sheba, she simply hasn't got 'em."

Clare went, sometimes with Irene and Brian, to parties and dances, and on a few occasions when Irene hadn't been able or inclined to go out, she had gone alone with Brian to some bridge party or benefit dance.

Once in a while she came formally to dine with them. She wasn't, however, in spite of her poise and air of worldliness, the ideal dinner-party guest. Beyond the æsthetic pleasure one got from watching her, she contributed little, sitting for the most part silent, an odd dreaming look in her hypnotic eyes. Though she could for some purpose of her own—the desire to be included in some party being made up to go cabareting, or an invitation to a dance or a tea—talk fluently and entertainingly.

She was generally liked. She was so friendly and responsive, and so ready to press the sweet food of flattery on all. Nor did she object to appearing a bit pathetic and ill-used, so that people could feel sorry for her. And, no matter how often she came among them, she still remained someone apart, a little mysterious and strange, someone to wonder about and to admire and to pity.

Her visits were undecided and uncertain, being, as they were, dependent on the presence or absence of John Bellew in the city. But she did, once in a while, manage to steal uptown for an afternoon even when he was not away. As time went on without any apparent danger of discovery, even Irene ceased to be perturbed about the possibility of Clare's husband's stumbling on her racial identity.

The daughter, Margery, had been left in Switzerland in school, for Clare and Bellew would be going back in the early spring. In March, Clare thought. "And how I do hate to think of it!" she would say, always with a suggestion of leashed rebellion; "but I can't see how I'm going to get out of it. Jack won't hear of my staying behind. If I could have just a couple of months more in New York, alone I mean, I'd be the happiest thing in the world."

"I imagine you'll be happy enough, once you get away," Irene told her one day when she was bewailing her approaching departure. "Remember, there's Margery. Think how glad you'll be to see her after all this time."

"Children aren't everything," was Clare Kendry's

answer to that. "There are other things in the world, though I admit some people don't seem to suspect it." And she laughed, more, it seemed, at some secret joke of her own than at her words.

Irene replied: "You know you don't mean that, Clare. You're only trying to tease me. I know very well that I take being a mother rather seriously. I *am* wrapped up in my boys and the running of my house. I can't help it. And, really, I don't think it's anything to laugh at." And though she was aware of the slight primness in her words and attitude, she had neither power nor wish to efface it.

Clare, suddenly very sober and sweet, said: "You're right. It's no laughing matter. It's shameful of me to tease you, 'Rene. You are so good." And she reached out and gave Irene's hand an affectionate little squeeze. "Don't think," she added, "whatever happens, that I'll ever forget how good you've been to me."

"Nonsense!"

"Oh, but you have, you have. It's just that I haven't any proper morals or sense of duty, as you have, that makes me act as I do."

"Now you are talking nonsense."

"But it's true, 'Rene. Can't you realize that I'm not like you a bit? Why, to get the things I want badly

enough, I'd do anything, hurt anybody, throw anything away. Really, 'Rene, I'm not safe." Her voice as
well as the look on her face had a beseeching earnest-
ness that made Irene vaguely uncomfortable.

She said: "I don't believe it. In the first place what
you're saying is so utterly, so wickedly wrong. And as
for your giving up things—" She stopped, at a loss for
an acceptable term to express her opinion of Clare's
"having" nature.

But Clare Kendry had begun to cry, audibly, with
no effort at restraint, and for no reason that Irene
could discover.

PART THREE

FINALE

ONE

The year was getting on towards its end. October, November had gone. December had come and brought with it a little snow and then a freeze and after that a thaw and some soft pleasant days that had in them a feeling of spring.

It wasn't, this mild weather, a bit Christmasy, Irene Redfield was thinking, as she turned out of Seventh Avenue into her own street. She didn't like it to be warm and springy when it should have been cold and crisp, or grey and cloudy as if snow was about to fall. The weather, like people, ought to enter into the spirit of the season. Here the holidays were almost upon them, and the streets through which she had come were streaked with rills of muddy water and the sun shone so warmly that children had taken off their hats and scarfs. It was all as soft, as like April, as possible. The kind of weather for Easter. Certainly not for Christmas.

Though, she admitted, reluctantly, she herself didn't feel the proper Christmas spirit this year, either. But that couldn't be helped, it seemed, any more than the weather. She was weary and depressed. And for all her trying, she couldn't be free of that dull, indefinite misery which with increasing tenaciousness had laid hold of her. The morning's aimless wandering through the teeming Harlem streets, long after she had ordered the flowers which had been her excuse for setting out, was but another effort to tear herself loose from it.

She went up the cream stone steps, into the house, and down to the kitchen. There were to be people in to tea. But that, she found, after a few words with Sadie and Zulena, need give her no concern. She was thankful. She didn't want to be bothered. She went upstairs and took off her things and got into bed.

She thought: "Bother those people coming to tea!"

She thought: "If I could only be sure that at bottom it's just Brazil."

She thought: "Whatever it is, if I only knew what it was, I could manage it."

Brian again. Unhappy, restless, withdrawn. And she, who had prided herself on knowing his moods, their causes and their remedies, had found it first unthinkable, and then intolerable, that this, so like and yet so unlike those other spasmodic restlessnesses of his, should be to her incomprehensible and elusive.

He was restless and he was not restless. He was discontented, yet there were times when she felt he was possessed of some intense secret satisfaction, like a cat who had stolen the cream. He was irritable with the boys, especially Junior, for Ted, who seemed to have an uncanny knowledge of his father's periods of off moods, kept out of his way when possible. They got on his nerves, drove him to violent outbursts of temper, very different from his usual gently sarcastic remarks that constituted his idea of discipline for them. On the other hand, with her he was more than customarily considerate and abstemious. And it had been weeks since she had felt the keen edge of his irony.

He was like a man marking time, waiting. But what was he waiting for? It was extraordinary that, after all these years of accurate perception, she now lacked the talent to discover what that appearance of waiting meant. It was the knowledge that, for all her watching, all her patient study, the reason for his humour still eluded her which filled her with foreboding dread. That guarded reserve of his seemed to her unjust, inconsiderate, and alarming. It was as if he had stepped out beyond her reach into some section, strange and walled, where she could not get at him.

She closed her eyes, thinking what a blessing it would be if she could get a little sleep before the boys came in from school. She couldn't, of course, though she was so tired, having had, of late, so many sleepless nights. Nights filled with questionings and premonitions.

But she did sleep—several hours.

She wakened to find Brian standing at her bedside looking down at her, an unfathomable expression in his eyes.

She said: "I must have dropped off to sleep," and watched a slender ghost of his old amused smile pass over his face.

"It's getting on to four," he told her, meaning, she knew, that she was going to be late again.

She fought back the quick answer that rose to her lips and said instead: "I'm getting right up. It was good of you to think to call me." She sat up.

He bowed. "Always the attentive husband, you see."

"Yes indeed. Thank goodness, everything's ready."

"Except you. Oh, and Clare's downstairs."

"Clare! What a nuisance! I didn't ask her. Purposely."

"I see. Might a mere man ask why? Or is the reason so subtly feminine that it wouldn't be understood by him?"

A little of his smile had come back. Irene, who was beginning to shake off some of her depression under his familiar banter, said, almost gaily: "Not at all. It just happens that this party happens to be for Hugh, and that Hugh happens not to care a great deal for Clare; therefore I, who happen to be giving the party, didn't happen to ask her. Nothing could be simpler. Could it?"

"Nothing. It's so simple that I can easily see beyond your simple explanation and surmise that Clare, probably, just never happened to pay Hugh the admiring attention that he happens to consider no more than his just due. Simplest thing in the world."

Irene exclaimed in amazement: "Why, I thought you liked Hugh! You don't, you can't, believe anything so idiotic!"

"Well, Hugh does think he's God, you know."

"That," Irene declared, getting out of bed, "is absolutely not true. He thinks ever so much better of himself than that, as you, who know and have read him, ought to be able to guess. If you remember what a low opinion he has of God, you won't make such a silly mistake."

She went into the closet for her things and, coming back, hung her frock over the back of a chair and placed her shoes on the floor beside it. Then she sat down before her dressing-table.

Brian didn't speak. He continued to stand beside the bed, seeming to look at nothing in particular. Certainly not at her. True, his gaze was on her, but in it there was some quality that made her feel that at that moment she was no more to him than a pane of glass through which he stared. At what? She didn't know, couldn't guess. And this made her uncomfortable. Piqued her.

She said: "It just happens that Hugh prefers intelligent women."

Plainly he was startled. "D'you mean that you think Clare is stupid?" he asked, regarding her with lifted eyebrows, which emphasized the disbelief of his voice.

She wiped the cold cream from her face, before she

said: "No, I don't. She isn't stupid. She's intelligent enough in a purely feminine way. Eighteenth-century France would have been a marvellous setting for her, or the old South if she hadn't made the mistake of being born a Negro."

"I see. Intelligent enough to wear a tight bodice and keep bowing swains whispering compliments and retrieving dropped fans. Rather a pretty picture. I take it, though, as slightly feline in its implication."

"Well, then, all I can say is that you take it wrongly. Nobody admires Clare more than I do, for the kind of intelligence she has, as well as for her decorative qualities. But she's not—She isn't— She hasn't— Oh, I can't explain it. Take Bianca, for example, or, to keep to the race, Felise Freeland. Looks *and* brains. Real brains that can hold their own with anybody. Clare has got brains of a sort, the kind that are useful too. Acquisitive, you know. But she'd bore a man like Hugh to suicide. Still, I never thought that even Clare would come to a private party to which she hadn't been asked. But, it's like her."

For a minute there was silence. She completed the bright red arch of her full lips. Brian moved towards the door. His hand was on the knob. He said: "I'm sorry, Irene. It's my fault entirely. She seemed so hurt

at being left out that I told her I was sure you'd forgotten and to just come along."

Irene cried out: "But, Brian, I—" and stopped,
amazed at the fierce anger that had blazed up in her.

Brian's head came round with a jerk. His brows
lifted in an odd surprise.

Her voice, she realized, *had* gone queer. But she
had an instinctive feeling that it hadn't been the
whole cause of his attitude. And that little straighten-
ing motion of the shoulders. Hadn't it been like that
of a man drawing himself up to receive a blow? Her
fright was like a scarlet spear of terror leaping at her
heart.

Clare Kendry! So that was it! Impossible. It couldn't
be.

In the mirror before her she saw that he was still
regarding her with that air of slight amazement. She
dropped her eyes to the jars and bottles on the table
and began to fumble among them with hands whose
fingers shook slightly.

"Of course," she said carefully, "I'm glad you did.
And in spite of my recent remarks, Clare does add to
any party. She's so easy on the eyes."

When she looked again, the surprise had gone from
his face and the expectancy from his bearing.

"Yes," he agreed. "Well, I guess I'll run along. One of us ought to be down, I s'pose."

"You're right. One of us ought to." She was surprised that it was in her normal tones she spoke, caught as she was by the heart since that dull indefinite fear had grown suddenly into sharp panic. "I'll be down before you know it," she promised.

"All right." But he still lingered. "You're quite certain. You don't mind my asking her? Not awfully, I mean? I see now that I ought to have spoken to you. Trust women to have their reasons for everything."

She made a little pretence at looking at him, managed a tiny smile, and turned away. Clare! How sickening!

"Yes, don't they?" she said, striving to keep her voice casual. Within her she felt a hardness from feeling, not absent, but repressed. And that hardness was rising, swelling. Why didn't he go? Why didn't he?

He had opened the door at last. "You won't be long?" he asked, admonished.

She shook her head, unable to speak, for there was a choking in her throat, and the confusion in her mind was like the beating of wings. Behind her she heard the gentle impact of the door as it closed behind him, and knew that he had gone. Down to Clare.

For a long minute she sat in strained stiffness. The face in the mirror vanished from her sight, blotted out by this thing which had so suddenly flashed across her groping mind. Impossible for her to put it immediately into words or give it outline, for, prompted by some impulse of self-protection, she recoiled from exact expression.

She closed her unseeing eyes and clenched her fists. She tried not to cry. But her lips tightened and no effort could check the hot tears of rage and shame that sprang into her eyes and flowed down her cheeks; so she laid her face in her arms and wept silently.

When she was sure that she had done crying, she wiped away the warm remaining tears and got up. After bathing her swollen face in cold, refreshing water and carefully applying a stinging splash of toilet water, she went back to the mirror and regarded herself gravely. Satisfied that there lingered no betraying evidence of weeping, she dusted a little powder on her dark-white face and again examined it carefully, and with a kind of ridiculing contempt.

"I do think," she confided to it, "that you've been something—oh, very much—of a damned fool."

Downstairs the ritual of tea gave her some busy moments, and that, she decided, was a blessing. She wanted no empty spaces of time in which her mind would immediately return to that horror which she had not yet gathered sufficient courage to face. Pouring tea properly and nicely was an occupation that required a kind of well-balanced attention.

In the room beyond, a clock chimed. A single sound. Fifteen minutes past five o'clock. That was all! And yet in the short space of half an hour all of life had changed, lost its colour, its vividness, its whole meaning. No, she reflected, it wasn't that that had happened. Life about her, apparently, went on exactly as before.

"Oh, Mrs. Runyon.... So nice to see you.... Two?... Really?... How exciting!... Yes, I think Tuesday's all right...."

Yes, life went on precisely as before. It was only she that had changed. Knowing, stumbling on this thing, had changed her. It was as if in a house long dim, a match had been struck, showing ghastly shapes where had been only blurred shadows.

Chatter, chatter, chatter. Someone asked her a question. She glanced up with what she felt was a rigid smile.

"Yes... Brian picked it up last winter in Haiti. Terribly weird, isn't it?... It *is* rather marvellous in its own hideous way.... Practically nothing, I believe. A few cents...."

Hideous. A great weariness came over her. Even the small exertion of pouring golden tea into thin old cups seemed almost too much for her. She went on pouring. Made repetitions of her smile. Answered questions. Manufactured conversation. She thought: "I feel like the oldest person in the world with the longest stretch of life before me."

"Josephine Baker?[1] . . . No. I've never seen her. . . . Well, she might have been in *Shuffle Along*[2] when I saw it, but if she was, I don't remember her. . . . Oh, but you're wrong! . . . I do think Ethel Waters[3] is awfully good. . . ."

There were the familiar little tinkling sounds of spoons striking against frail cups, the soft running sounds of inconsequential talk, punctuated now and then with laughter. In irregular small groups, disintegrating, coalescing, striking just the right note of disharmony, disorder in the big room, which Irene had furnished with a sparingness that was almost chaste, moved the guests with that slight familiarity that makes a party a success. On the floor and the walls the sinking sun threw long, fantastic shadows.

So like many other tea-parties she had had. So unlike any of those others. But she mustn't think yet. Time enough for that after. All the time in the world.

She had a second's flashing knowledge of what those words might portend. Time with Brian. Time without him. It was gone, leaving in its place an almost uncontrollable impulse to laugh, to scream, to hurl things about. She wanted, suddenly, to shock people, to hurt them, to make them notice her, to be aware of her suffering.

"Hello, Dave. . . . Felise. . . . Really your clothes are the despair of half the women in Harlem. . . . How do you do it? . . . Lovely, is it Worth or Lanvin? . . . Oh, a mere Babani. . . ."[4]

"Merely that," Felise Freeland acknowledged. "Come out of it, Irene, whatever it is. You look like the second gravedigger."

"Thanks, for the hint, Felise. I'm not feeling quite up to par. The weather, I guess."

"Buy yourself an expensive new frock, child. It always helps. Any time this child gets the blues, it means money out of Dave's pocket. How're those boys of yours?"

The boys! For once she'd forgotten them.

They were, she told Felise, very well. Felise mumbled something about that being awfully nice, and said she'd have to fly, because for a wonder she saw Mrs. Bellew sitting by herself, "and I've been trying to get her alone all afternoon. I want her for a party. Isn't she stunning today?"

Clare was. Irene couldn't remember ever having seen her look better. She was wearing a superlatively simple cinnamon-brown frock which brought out all her vivid beauty, and a little golden bowl of a hat. Around her neck hung a string of amber beads that would easily have made six or eight like one Irene owned. Yes, she was stunning.

The ripple of talk flowed on. The fire roared. The shadows stretched longer.

Across the room was Hugh. He wasn't, Irene hoped, being too bored. He seemed as he always did, a bit aloof, a little amused, and somewhat weary. And as usual he was hovering before the book-shelves. But he was not, she noticed, looking at the book he had taken down. Instead, his dull amber eyes were held by something across the room. They were a little scornful. Well, Hugh had never cared for Clare Kendry. For a minute Irene hesitated, then turned her head, though she knew what it was that held Hugh's gaze. Clare, who had suddenly clouded all her days. Brian, the father of Ted and Junior.

Clare's ivory face was what it always was, beautiful and caressing. Or maybe today a little masked. Unrevealing. Unaltered and undisturbed by any emotion within or without. Brian's seemed to Irene to be pitiably bare. Or was it too as it always was? That half-effaced seeking look, did he always have that? Queer, that now she didn't know, couldn't recall. Then she saw him smile, and the smile made his face all eager and shining. Impelled by some inner urge of loyalty to herself, she glanced away. But only for a moment. And when she turned towards them again, she thought that the look on his face was the most melancholy and yet the most scoffing that she had ever seen upon it.

In the next quarter of an hour she promised herself to Bianca Wentworth in Sixty-second Street, Jane Tenant at Seventh Avenue and a Hundred and Fiftieth Street, and the Dashields in Brooklyn for dinner all on the same evening and at almost the same hour.

Oh well, what did it matter? She had no thoughts at all now, and all she felt was a great fatigue. Before her tired eyes Clare Kendry was talking to Dave Freeland.[5] Scraps of their conversation, in Clare's husky voice, floated over to her: ". . . always admired you . . . so much about you long ago . . . everybody says so . . . no one but you. . . ." And more of the same. The man hung rapt on her words, though he was the husband of Felise Freeland, and the author of novels that revealed a man of perception and a devastating irony. And he fell for such pish-posh! And all because Clare had a trick of sliding down ivory lids over astonishing black eyes and then lifting them suddenly and turning on a caressing smile. Men like Dave Freeland fell for it. And Brian.

Her mental and physical languor receded. Brian. What did it mean? How would it affect her and the boys? The boys! She had a surge of relief. It ebbed, vanished. A feeling of absolute unimportance followed. Actually, she didn't count. She was, to him, only the mother of his sons. That was all. Alone she was nothing. Worse. An obstacle.

Rage boiled up in her.

There was a slight crash. On the floor at her feet lay the shattered cup. Dark stains dotted the bright rug. Spread. The chatter stopped. Went on. Before her, Zulena gathered up the white fragments.

As from a distance Hugh Wentworth's clipt voice came to her, though he was, she was aware, somehow miraculously at her side. "Sorry," he apologized. "Must have pushed you. Clumsy of me. Don't tell me it's priceless and irreplaceable."

It hurt. Dear God! How the thing hurt! But she

couldn't think of that now. Not with High sitting there mumbling apologies and lies. The significance of his words, the power of his discernment, stirred in her a sense of caution. Her pride revolted. Damn Hugh! Something would have to be done about him. Now. She couldn't, it seemed, help his knowing. It was too late for that. But she could and would keep him from knowing that she knew. She could, she would bear it. She'd have to. There were the boys. Her whole body went taut. In that second she saw that she could bear anything, but only if no one knew that she had anything to bear. It hurt. It frightened her, but she could bear it.

She turned to Hugh. Shook her head. Raised innocent dark eyes to his concerned pale ones. "Oh, no," she protested, "you didn't push me. Cross your heart, hope to die, and I'll tell you how it happened."

"Done!"

"Did you notice that cup? Well, you're lucky. It was the ugliest thing that your ancestors, the charming Confederates ever owned. I've forgotten how many thousands of years ago it was that Brian's great-great-grand-uncle owned it. But it has, or had, a good old hoary history. It was brought North by way of the subway. Oh, all right! Be English if you want to and call it the underground.[6] What I'm coming to is the fact that I've never figured out a way of getting rid of it until about five minutes ago. I had an inspiration. I had only to break it, and I was rid of it for ever. So simple! And I'd never thought of it before."

Hugh nodded and his frosty smile spread over his features. Had she convinced him?

"Still," she went on with a little laugh that didn't, she was sure, sound the least bit forced, "I'm perfectly willing for you to take the blame and admit that you pushed me at the wrong moment. What are friends for, if not to help bear our sins? Brian will certainly be told that it was your fault.

"More tea, Clare? . . . I haven't had a minute with you. . . . Yes, it is a nice party. . . . You'll stay to dinner, I hope. . . . Oh, too bad! . . . I'll be alone with the boys. . . . They'll be sorry. Brian's got a medical meeting, or something. . . . Nice frock you're wearing. . . . Thanks. . . . Well, good-bye; see you soon, I hope."

The clock chimed. One. Two. Three. Four. Five. Six. Was it, could it be, only a little over an hour since she had come down to tea? One little hour.

"Must you go? . . . Good-bye. . . . Thank you so much. . . . So nice to see you. . . . Yes, Wednesday. . . . My love to Madge. . . . Sorry, but I'm filled up for Tuesday. . . . Oh, really? . . . Yes. . . . Good-bye. . . . Good-bye. . . ."

It hurt. It hurt like hell. But it didn't matter, if no one knew. If everything could go on as before. If the boys were safe.

It did hurt.

But it didn't matter.

TWO

But it did matter. It mattered more than anything had ever mattered before.

What bitterness! That the one fear, the one uncertainty, that she had felt, Brian's ache to go somewhere else, should have dwindled to a childish triviality! And with it the quality of the courage and resolution with which she had met it. From the visions and dangers which she now perceived she shrank away. For them she had no remedy or courage. Desperately she tried to shut out the knowledge from which had risen this turmoil, which she had no power to moderate or still, within her. And half succeeded.

For, she reasoned, what was there, what had there been, to show that she was even half correct in her tormenting notion? Nothing. She had seen nothing, heard nothing. She had no facts or proofs. She was only making herself unutterably wretched by an unfounded suspicion. It had been a case of looking for trouble and finding it in good measure. Merely that.

With this self-assurance that she had no real knowledge, she redoubled her efforts to drive out of her mind the distressing thought of faiths broken and trusts betrayed which every mental vision of Clare, of Brian, brought with them. She could not, she would not, go again through the tearing agony that lay just behind her.

She must, she told herself, be fair. In all their married life she had had no slightest cause to suspect her husband of any infidelity, of any serious flirtation even. If—and she doubted it—he had had his hours of outside erratic conduct, they were unknown to her. Why begin now to assume them? And on nothing more concrete than an idea that had leapt into her mind because he had told her that he had invited a friend, a friend of hers, to a party in his own house. And at a time when she had been, it was likely, more asleep than awake. How could she without anything done or said, or left undone or unsaid, so easily believe him guilty? How be so ready to renounce all confidence in the worth of their life together?

And if, perchance, there were some small something—well, what could it mean? Nothing. There were the boys. There was John Bellew. The thought of these three gave her some slight relief. But she did not look the future in the face. She wanted to feel nothing, to think nothing; simply to believe that it was all silly invention on her part. Yet she could not. Not quite.

———

Christmas, with its unreality, its hectic rush, its false gaiety, came and went. Irene was thankful for the confused unrest of the season. Its irksomeness, its crowds, its inane and insincere repetitions of genialities, pushed between her and the contemplation of her growing unhappiness.

She was thankful, too, for the continued absence of Clare, who, John Bellew having returned from a long stay in Canada, had withdrawn to that other life of hers, remote and inaccessible. But beating against the walled prison of Irene's thoughts was the shunned fancy that, though absent, Clare Kendry was still present, that she was close.

Brian, too, had withdrawn. The house contained

his outward self and his belongings. He came and went with his usual noiseless irregularity. He sat across from her at table. He slept in his room next to hers at night.[1] But he was remote and inaccessible. No use pretending that he was happy, that things were the same as they had always been. He wasn't and they weren't. However, she assured herself, it needn't necessarily be because of anything that involved Clare. It was, it must be, another manifestation of the old longing.

But she did wish it were spring, March, so that Clare would be sailing, out of her life and Brian's. Though she had come almost to believe that there was nothing but generous friendship between those two, she was very tired of Clare Kendry. She wanted to be free of her, and of her furtive comings and goings. If something would only happen, something that would make John Bellew decide on an earlier departure, or that would remove Clare. Anything. She didn't care what. Not even if it were that Clare's Margery were ill, or dying. Not even if Bellew should discover—

She drew a quick, sharp breath. And for a long time sat staring down at the hands in her lap. Strange, she had not before realized how easily she could put Clare out of her life! She had only to tell John Bellew that his wife—No. Not that! But if he should somehow learn of these Harlem visits— Why should she hesitate? Why spare Clare?

But she shrank away from the idea of telling that man, Clare Kendry's white husband, anything that would lead him to suspect that his wife was a Negro. Nor could she write it, or telephone it, or tell it to someone else who would tell him.

She was caught between two allegiances, different, yet the same. Herself. Her race. Race! The thing that bound and suffocated her. Whatever steps she took, or if she took none at all, something would be crushed. A person or the race. Clare, herself, or the race. Or, it might be, all three. Nothing, she imagined, was ever more completely sardonic.

Sitting alone in the quiet living-room in the pleasant firelight, Irene Redfield wished, for the first time in her life, that she had not been born a Negro. For the first time she suffered and rebelled because she was unable to disregard the burden of race. It was, she cried silently, enough to suffer as a woman, an individual, on one's own account, without having to suffer for the race as well. It was a brutality, and undeserved. Surely, no other people so cursed as Ham's dark children.[2]

Nevertheless, her weakness, her shrinking, her

own inability to compass the thing, did not prevent her from wishing fervently that, in some way with which she had no concern, John Bellew would discover, not that his wife had a touch of the tar-brush—Irene didn't want that—but that she was spending all the time that he was out of the city in black Harlem. Only that. It would be enough to rid her forever of Clare Kendry.

THREE

As if in answer to her wish, the very next day Irene came face to face with Bellew.

She had gone downtown with Felise Freeland to shop. The day was an exceptionally cold one, with a strong wind that had whipped a dusky red into Felise's smooth golden cheeks and driven moisture into Irene's soft brown eyes.

Clinging to each other, with heads bent against the wind, they turned out of the Avenue[1] into Fifty-seventh Street. A sudden bluster flung them around the corner with unexpected quickness and they collided with a man.

"Pardon," Irene begged laughingly, and looked up into the face of Clare Kendry's husband.

"Mrs. Redfield!"

His hat came off. He held out his hand, smiling genially.

But the smile faded at once. Surprise, incredulity, and—was it understanding?—passed over his features.

He had, Irene knew, become conscious of Felise, golden, with curly black Negro hair, whose arm was still linked in her own. She was sure, now, of the understanding in his face, as he looked at her again and then back at Felise. And displeasure.

He didn't, however, withdraw his outstretched hand. Not at once.

But Irene didn't take it. Instinctively, in the first glance of recognition, her face had become a mask. Now she turned on him a totally uncomprehending look, a bit questioning. Seeing that he still stood with hand outstretched, she gave him the cool appraising stare which she reserved for mashers,[2] and drew Felise on.

Felise drawled: "Aha! Been 'passing,' have you? Well, I've queered[3] that."

"Yes, I'm afraid you have."

"Why, Irene Redfield! You sound as if you cared terribly. I'm sorry."

"I do, but not for the reason you think. I don't believe I've ever gone native[4] in my life except for the sake of convenience, restaurants, theatre tickets, and things like that. Never socially I mean, except once. You've just passed the only person that I've ever met disguised as a white woman."

"Awfully sorry. Be sure your sin will find you out and all that. Tell me about it."

"I'd like to. It would amuse you. But I can't."

Felise's laughter was as languidly nonchalant as her cool voice. "Can it be possible that the honest Irene has— Oh, do look at that coat! There. The red one. Isn't it a dream?"

Irene was thinking: "I had my chance and didn't take it. I had only to speak and to introduce him to Felise with the casual remark that he was Clare's husband. Only that. Fool. Fool." That instinctive loyalty to a race. Why couldn't she get free of it? Why should it include Clare? Clare, who'd shown little enough consideration for her, and hers. What she felt was not so much resentment as a dull despair because she could not change herself in this respect, could not separate individuals from the race, herself from Clare Kendry.

"Let's go home, Felise. I'm so tired I could drop."

"Why, we haven't done half the things we planned."

"I know, but it's too cold to be running all over town. But you stay down if you want to."

"I think I'll do that, if you don't mind."

———

And now another problem confronted Irene. She must tell Clare of this meeting. Warn her. But how? She hadn't seen her for days. Writing and telephoning were equally unsafe. And even if it was possible to get in touch with her, what good would it do? If Bellew hadn't concluded that he'd made a mistake, if he was certain of her identity—and he was nobody's fool—telling Clare wouldn't avert the results of the encounter. Besides, it was too late. Whatever was in store for Clare Kendry had already overtaken her.

Irene was conscious of a feeling of relieved thankfulness at the thought that she was probably rid of Clare, and without having lifted a finger or uttered one word.

But she did mean to tell Brian about meeting John Bellew.

But that, it seemed, was impossible. Strange. Something held her back. Each time she was on the verge of saying: "I ran into Clare's husband on the street downtown today. I'm sure he recognized me, and Felise was with me," she failed to speak. It sounded too much like the warning she wanted it to be. Not even in the presence of the boys at dinner could she make the bare statement.

The evening dragged. At last she said good-night and went upstairs, the words unsaid.

She thought: "Why didn't I tell him? Why didn't I? If trouble comes from this, I'll never forgive myself. I'll tell him when he comes up."

She took up a book, but she could not read, so oppressed was she by a nameless foreboding.

What if Bellew should divorce Clare? Could he? There was the Rhinelander case.[5] But in France, in Paris, such things were very easy. If he divorced her—If Clare were free—But of all the things that could happen, that was the one she did not want. She must get her mind away from that possibility. She must.

Then came a thought which she tried to drive away. If Clare should die! Then— Oh, it was vile! To think, yes, to wish that! She felt faint and sick. But the thought stayed with her. She could not get rid of it.

She heard the outer door open. Close. Brian had gone out. She turned her face into her pillow to cry. But no tears came.

She lay there awake, thinking of things past. Of her

courtship and marriage and Junior's birth. Of the time they had bought the house in which they had lived so long and so happily. Of the time Ted had passed his pneumonia crisis and they knew he would live. And of other sweet painful memories that would never come again.

Above everything else she had wanted, had striven, to keep undisturbed the pleasant routine of her life. And now Clare Kendry had come into it, and with her the menace of impermanence.

"Dear God," she prayed, "make March come quickly."

By and by she slept.

FOUR

The next morning brought with it a snowstorm that lasted throughout the day.

After a breakfast, which had been eaten almost in silence and which she was relieved to have done with, Irene Redfield lingered for a little while in the downstairs hall, looking out at the soft flakes fluttering down. She was watching them immediately fill some ugly irregular gaps left by the feet of hurrying pedestrians when Zulena came to her, saying: "The telephone, Mrs. Redfield. It's Mrs. Bellew."

"Take the message, Zulena, please."

Though she continued to stare out of the window, Irene saw nothing now, stabbed as she was by fear—

and hope. Had anything happened between Clare and Bellew? And if so, what? And was she to be freed at last from the aching anxiety of the past weeks? Or was there to be more, and worse? She had a wrestling moment, in which it seemed that she must rush after Zulena and hear for herself what it was that Clare had to say. But she waited.

Zulena, when she came back, said: "She says, ma'am, that she'll be able to go to Mrs. Freeland's tonight. She'll be here some time between eight and nine."

"Thank you, Zulena."

The day dragged on to its end.

At dinner Brian spoke bitterly of a lynching that he had been reading about in the evening paper.

"Dad, why is it that they only lynch coloured people?" Ted asked.

"Because they hate 'em, son."

"Brian!" Irene's voice was a plea and a rebuke.

Ted said: "Oh! And why do they hate 'em?"

"Because they are afraid of them."

"But what makes them afraid of 'em?"

"Because—"

"Brian!"

"It seems, son, that is a subject we can't go into at the moment without distressing the ladies of our family," he told the boy with mock seriousness, "but we'll take it up some time when we're alone together."

Ted nodded in his engaging grave way. "I see. Maybe we can talk about it tomorrow on the way to school."

"That'll be fine."

"Brian!"

"Mother," Junior remarked, "that's the third time you've said 'Brian' like that."

"But not the last, Junior, never you fear," his father told him.

After the boys had gone up to their own floor, Irene said suavely: "I do wish, Brian, that you wouldn't talk about lynching before Ted and Junior. It was really inexcusable for you to bring up a thing like that at dinner. There'll be time enough for them to learn about such horrible things when they're older."

"You're absolutely wrong! If, as you're so determined, they've got to live in this damned country, they'd better find out what sort of thing they're up against as soon as possible. The earlier they learn it, the better prepared they'll be."

"I don't agree. I want their childhood to be happy and as free from the knowledge of such things as it possibly can be."

"Very laudable," was Brian's sarcastic answer. "Very laudable indeed, all things considered. But can it?"

"Certainly it can. If you'll only do your part."

"Stuff! You know as well as I do, Irene, that it can't. What was the use of our trying to keep them from learning the word 'nigger' and its connotation? They found out, didn't they? And how? Because somebody called Junior a dirty nigger."

"Just the same you're not to talk to them about the race problem. I won't have it."

They glared at each other.

"I tell you, Irene, they've got to know these things, and it might as well be now as later."

"They do not!" she insisted, forcing back the tears of anger that were threatening to fall.

Brian growled: "I can't understand how anybody as intelligent as you like to think you are can show evidences of such stupidity." He looked at her in a puzzled harassed way.

"Stupid!" she cried. "Is it stupid to want my children to be happy?" Her lips were quivering.

"At the expense of proper preparation for life and their future happiness, yes. And I'd feel I hadn't done my duty by them if I didn't give them some inkling of what's before them. It's the least I can do. I wanted to get them out of this hellish place years ago. You wouldn't let me. I gave up the idea, because you objected. Don't expect me to give up everything."

Under the lash of his words she was silent. Before any answer came to her, he had turned and gone from the room.

Sitting there alone in the forsaken dining-room, unconsciously pressing the hands lying in her lap, tightly together, she was seized by a convulsion of shivering. For, to her, there had been something ominous in the scene that she had just had with her husband. Over and over in her mind his last words: "Don't expect me to give up everything," repeated themselves. What had they meant? What could they mean? Clare Kendry?

Surely, she was going mad with fear and suspicion. She must not work herself up. She must not! Where were all the self-control, the common sense, that she was so proud of? Now, if ever, was the time for it.

Clare would soon be there. She must hurry or she would be late again, and those two would wait for her downstairs together, as they had done so often since that first time, which now seemed so long ago. Had it been really only last October? Why, she felt years, not months, older.

Drearily she rose from her chair and went upstairs

to set about the business of dressing to go out when she would far rather have remained at home. During the process she wondered, for the hundredth time, why she hadn't told Brian about herself and Felise running into Bellew the day before, and for the hundredth time she turned away from acknowledging to herself the real reason for keeping back the information.

When Clare arrived, radiant in a shining red gown, Irene had not finished dressing. But her smile scarcely hesitated as she greeted her, saying: "I always seem to keep C. P. time,[1] don't I? We hardly expected you to be able to come. Felise will be pleased. How nice you look."

Clare kissed a bare shoulder, seeming not to notice a slight shrinking.

"I hadn't an idea in the world, myself, that I'd be able to make it; but Jack had to run down to Philadelphia unexpectedly. So here I am."

Irene looked up, a flood of speech on her lips. "Philadelphia. That's not very far, is it? Clare, I—?"

She stopped, one of her hands clutching the side of her stool, the other lying clenched on the dressing-table. Why didn't she go on and tell Clare about meeting Bellew? Why couldn't she?

But Clare didn't notice the unfinished sentence.

She laughed and said lightly: "It's far enough for me. Anywhere, away from me, is far enough. I'm not particular."

Irene passed a hand over her eyes to shut out the accusing face in the glass before her. With one corner of her mind she wondered how long she had looked like that, drawn and haggard and—yes, frightened. Or was it only imagination?

"Clare," she asked, "have you ever seriously thought what it would mean if he should find you out?"

"Yes."

"Oh! You have! And what you'd do in that case?"

"Yes." And having said it, Clare Kendry smiled quickly, a smile that came and went like a flash, leaving untouched the gravity of her face.

That smile and the quiet resolution of that one word, "yes," filled Irene with a primitive paralysing dread. Her hands were numb, her feet like ice, her heart like a stone weight. Even her tongue was like a heavy dying thing. There were long spaces between the words as she asked: "And what should you do?"

Clare, who was sunk in a deep chair, her eyes far away, seemed wrapped in some pleasant impenetrable reflection. To Irene, sitting expectantly upright, it was an interminable time before she dragged herself back to the present to say calmly: "I'd do what I want to do more than anything else right now. I'd come up here to live. Harlem, I mean. Then I'd be able to do as I please, when I please."

Irene leaned forward, cold and tense. "And what about Margery?" Her voice was a strained whisper.

"Margery?" Clare repeated, letting her eyes flutter over Irene's concerned face. "Just this, 'Rene. If it wasn't for her, I'd do it anyway. She's all that holds me back. But if Jack finds out, if our marriage is broken, that lets me out. Doesn't it?"

Her gentle resigned tone, her air of innocent candour, appeared, to her listener, spurious. A conviction that the words were intended as a warning took possession of Irene. She remembered that Clare Kendry had always seemed to know what other people were thinking. Her compressed lips grew firm and obdurate. Well, she wouldn't know this time.

She said: "Do go downstairs and talk to Brian. He's got a mad on."

Though she had determined that Clare should not get at her thoughts and fears, the words had sprung, unthought of, to her lips. It was as if they had come from some outer layer of callousness that had no relation to her tortured heart. And they had been, she realized, precisely the right words for her purpose.

For as Clare got up and went out, she saw that that arrangement was as good as her first plan of keeping her waiting up there while she dressed—or better. She would only have hindered and rasped her. And what matter if those two spent one hour, more or less, alone together, one or many, now that everything had happened between them?

Ah! The first time that she had allowed herself to admit to herself that everything had happened, had not forced herself to believe, to hope, that nothing irrevocable had been consummated! Well, it had happened. She knew it, and knew that she knew it.

She was surprised that, having thought the thought, conceded the fact, she was no more hurt, cared no more, than during her previous frenzied endeavours to escape it. And this absence of acute, unbearable pain seemed to her unjust, as if she had been denied some exquisite solace of suffering which the full acknowledgment should have given her.

Was it, perhaps, that she had endured all that a woman could endure of tormenting humiliation and fear? Or was it that she lacked the capacity for the acme of suffering? "No, no!" she denied fiercely. "I'm human like everybody else. It's just that I'm so tired, so worn out, I can't feel any more." But she did not really believe that.

Security. Was it just a word? If not, then was it only by the sacrifice of other things, happiness, love, or some wild ecstasy that she had never known, that it could be obtained? And did too much striving, too much faith in safety and permanence, unfit one for these other things?

Irene didn't know, couldn't decide, though for a long time she sat questioning and trying to understand. Yet all the while, in spite of her searchings and feeling of frustration, she was aware that, to her, security was the most important and desired thing in life. Not for any of the others, or for all of them, would she exchange it. She wanted only to be tranquil. Only, unmolested, to be allowed to direct for their own best good the lives of her sons and her husband.

Now that she had relieved herself of what was almost like a guilty knowledge, admitted that which by some sixth sense she had long known, she could again reach out for plans. Could think again of ways to keep Brian by her side, and in New York. For she would not go to Brazil. She belonged in this land of rising towers. She was an American. She grew from this soil, and she would not be uprooted. Not even because of Clare Kendry, or a hundred Clare Kendrys.

Brian, too, belonged here. His duty was to her and to his boys.

Strange, that she couldn't now be sure that she had ever truly known love. Not even for Brian. He was her husband and the father of her sons. But was he anything more? Had she ever wanted or tried for more? In that hour she thought not.

Nevertheless, she meant to keep him. Her freshly painted lips narrowed to a thin straight line. True, she had left off trying to believe that he and Clare loved and yet did not love, but she still intended to hold fast to the outer shell of her marriage, to keep her life fixed, certain. Brought to the edge of distasteful reality, her fastidious nature did not recoil. Better, far better, to share him than to lose him completely. Oh, she could close her eyes, if need be. She could bear it. She could bear anything. And there was March ahead. March and the departure of Clare.

Horribly clear, she could now see the reason for her instinct to withhold—omit, rather—her news of the encounter with Bellew. If Clare was freed, anything might happen.

She paused in her dressing, seeing with perfect clearness that dark truth which she had from that first

October afternoon felt about Clare Kendry and of which Clare herself had once warned her—that she got the things she wanted because she met the great condition of conquest, sacrifice. If she wanted Brian, Clare wouldn't revolt from the lack of money or place. It was as she had said, only Margery kept her from throwing all that away. And if things were taken out of her hands—Even if she was only alarmed, only suspected that such a thing was about to occur, anything might happen. Anything.

No! At all costs, Clare was not to know of that meeting with Bellew. Nor was Brian. It would only weaken her own power to keep him.

They would never know from her that he was on his way to suspecting the truth about his wife. And she would do anything, risk anything, to prevent him from finding out that truth. How fortunate that she had obeyed her instinct and omitted to recognize Bellew!

———

"Ever go up to the sixth floor, Clare?" Brian asked as he stopped the car and got out to open the door for them.

"Why, of course! We're on the seventeenth."

"I mean, did you ever go up by nigger-power?"[2]

"That's good!" Clare laughed. "Ask 'Rene. My father was a janitor, you know, in the good old days before every ramshackle flat had its elevator. But you can't mean we've got to walk up? Not here!"

"Yes, here. And Felise lives at the very top," Irene told her.

"What on earth for?"

"I believe she claims it discourages the casual visitor."

"And she's probably right. Hard on herself, though."

Brian said: "Yes, a bit. But she says she'd rather be dead than bored."

"Oh, a garden! And how lovely with that undisturbed snow!"

"Yes, isn't it? But keep to the walk with those foolish thin shoes. You too, Irene."

Irene walked beside them on the cleared cement path that split the whiteness of the courtyard garden. She felt a something in the air, something that had been between those two and would be again. It was like a live thing pressing against her. In a quick furtive glance she saw Clare clinging to Brian's other arm. She was looking at him with that provocative upward glance of hers, and his eyes were fastened on her face with what seemed to Irene an expression of wistful eagerness.

"It's this entrance, I believe," she informed them in quite her ordinary voice.

"Mind," Brian told Clare, "you don't fall by the wayside before the fourth floor. They absolutely refuse to carry anyone up more than the last two flights."

"Don't be silly!" Irene snapped.

———

The party began gaily.

Dave Freeland was at his best, brilliant, crystal clear, and sparkling. Felise, too, was amusing, and not so sarcastic as usual, because she liked the dozen or so guests that dotted the long, untidy living-room. Brian was witty, though, Irene noted, his remarks were somewhat more barbed than was customary even with him. And there was Ralph Hazelton, throwing nonsensical shining things into the pool of talk, which the others, even Clare, picked up and flung back with fresh adornment.

Only Irene wasn't merry. She sat almost silent, smiling now and then, that she might appear amused.

"What's the matter, Irene?" someone asked. "Taken a vow never to laugh, or something? You're as sober as a judge."

"No. It's simply that the rest of you are so clever that I'm speechless, absolutely stunned."

"No wonder," Dave Freeland remarked, "that you're on the verge of tears. You haven't a drink. What'll you take?"

"Thanks. If I must take something, make it a glass of ginger ale and three drops of Scotch. The Scotch first, please. Then the ice, then the ginger ale."

"Heavens! Don't attempt to mix that yourself, Dave darling. Have the butler in," Felise mocked.

"Yes, do. And the footman." Irene laughed a little, then said: "It seems dreadfully warm in here. Mind if I open this window?" With that she pushed open one of the long casement-windows of which the Free-lands were so proud.

It had stopped snowing some two or three hours back. The moon was just rising, and far behind the tall buildings a few stars were creeping out. Irene finished her cigarette and threw it out, watching the tiny spark drop slowly down to the white ground below.

Someone in the room had turned on the phono-graph. Or was it the radio? She didn't know which she disliked more. And nobody was listening to its blare. The talking, the laughter never for a minute ceased. Why must they have more noise?

Dave came with her drink. "You ought not," he told her, "to stand there like that. You'll take cold. Come along and talk to me, or listen to me gabble." Taking her arm, he led her across the room. They had just found seats when the door-bell rang and Felise called over to him to go and answer it.

In the next moment Irene heard his voice in the hall, carelessly polite: "Your wife? Sorry. I'm afraid you're wrong. Perhaps next—"

Then the roar of John Bellew's voice above all the other noises of the room: "I'm *not* wrong! I've been to the Redfields and I know she's with them. You'd better stand out of my way and save yourself trouble in the end."

"What is it, Dave?" Felise ran out to the door.

And so did Brian. Irene heard him saying: "I'm Redfield. What the devil's the matter with you?"

But Bellew didn't heed him. He pushed past them all into the room and strode towards Clare. They all looked at her as she got up from her chair, backing a little from his approach.

"So you're a nigger, a damned dirty nigger!" His voice was a snarl and a moan, an expression of rage and of pain.

Everything was in confusion. The men had sprung forward. Felise had leapt between them and Bellew. She said quickly: "Careful. You're the only white man here." And the silver chill of her voice, as well as her words, was a warning.

Clare stood at the window, as composed as if everyone were not staring at her in curiosity and wonder, as if the whole structure of her life were not lying in fragments before her. She seemed unaware of any danger or uncaring. There was even a faint smile on her full, red lips, and in her shining eyes.

It was that smile that maddened Irene. She ran across the room, her terror tinged with ferocity, and laid a hand on Clare's bare arm. One thought possessed her. She couldn't have Clare Kendry cast aside by Bellew. She couldn't have her free.

Before them stood John Bellew, speechless now in his hurt and anger. Beyond them the little huddle of other people, and Brian stepping out from among them.

What happened next, Irene Redfield never afterwards allowed herself to remember. Never clearly.

One moment Clare had been there, a vital glowing thing, like a flame of red and gold. The next she was gone.

There was a gasp of horror, and above it a sound not quite human, like a beast in agony. "Nig! My God! Nig!"

A frenzied rush of feet down long flights of stairs. The slamming of distant doors. Voices.

Irene stayed behind. She sat down and remained

quite still, staring at a ridiculous Japanese print on the wall across the room.

Gone! The soft white face, the bright hair, the disturbing scarlet mouth, the dreaming eyes, the caressing smile, the whole torturing loveliness that had been Clare Kendry. That beauty that had torn at Irene's placid life. Gone! The mocking daring, the gallantry of her pose, the ringing bells of her laughter.

Irene wasn't sorry. She was amazed, incredulous almost.

What would the others think? That Clare had fallen? That she had deliberately leaned backward? Certainly one or the other. Not—

But she mustn't, she warned herself, think of that. She was too tired, and too shocked. And, indeed, both were true. She was utterly weary, and she was violently staggered. But her thoughts reeled on. If only she could be as free of mental as she was of bodily vigour; could only put from her memory the vision of her hand on Clare's arm!

"It was an accident, a terrible accident," she muttered fiercely. "It *was.*"

People were coming up the stairs. Through the still open door their steps and talk sounded nearer, nearer.

Quickly she stood up and went noiselessly into the bedroom and closed the door softly behind her.

Her thoughts raced. Ought she to have stayed? Should she go back out there to them? But there would be questions. She hadn't thought of them, of afterwards, of this. She had thought of nothing in that sudden moment of action.

It was cold. Icy chills ran up her spine and over her bare neck and shoulders.

In the room outside there were voices. Dave Freeland's and others that she did not recognize.

Should she put on her coat? Felise had rushed down without any wrap. So had all the others. So had Brian. Brian! He mustn't take cold. She took up his coat and left her own. At the door she paused for a moment, listening fearfully. She heard nothing. No voices. No footsteps. Very slowly she opened the door. The room was empty. She went out.

In the hall below she heard dimly the sound of feet going down the steps, of a door being opened and closed, and of voices far away.

Down, down, down, she went, Brian's great coat clutched in her shivering arms and trailing a little on each step behind her.

What was she to say to them when at last she had

finished going down those endless stairs? She should
have rushed out when they did. What reason could
she give for her dallying behind? Even she didn't
know why she had done that. And what else would
she be asked? There had been her hand reaching out
towards Clare. What about that?

In the midst of her wonderings and questionings
came a thought so terrifying, so horrible, that she had
had to grasp hold of the banister to save herself from
pitching downwards. A cold perspiration drenched
her shaking body. Her breath came short in sharp and
painful gasps.

What if Clare was not dead?

She felt nauseated, as much at the idea of the glo-
rious body mutilated as from fear.

How she managed to make the rest of the journey
without fainting she never knew. But at last she was
down. Just at the bottom she came on the others, surrounded by a little circle of strangers. They were all
speaking in whispers, or in the awed, discreetly low-
ered tones adapted to the presence of disaster. In the
first instant she wanted to turn and rush back up the
way she had come. Then a calm desperation came
over her. She braced herself, physically and mentally.

"Here's Irene now," Dave Freeland announced,

and told her that, having only just missed her, they had concluded that she had fainted or something like that, and were on the way to find out about her. Felise, she saw, was holding on to his arm, all the insolent nonchalance gone out of her, and the golden brown of her handsome face changed to a queer mauve colour.

Irene made no indication that she had heard Freeland, but went straight to Brian. His face looked aged and altered, and his lips were purple and trembling. She had a great longing to comfort him, to charm away his suffering and horror. But she was helpless, having so completely lost control of his mind and heart.

She stammered: "Is she—is she—?"

It was Felise who answered. "Instantly, we think."

Irene struggled against the sob of thankfulness that rose in her throat. Choked down, it turned to a whimper, like a hurt child's. Someone laid a hand on her shoulder in a soothing gesture. Brian wrapped his coat about her. She began to cry rackingly, her entire body heaving with convulsive sobs. He made a slight perfunctory attempt to comfort her.

"There, there, Irene. You mustn't. You'll make yourself sick. She's—" His voice broke suddenly.

As from a long distance she heard Ralph Hazelton's voice saying: "I was looking right at her. She just tumbled over and was gone before you could say 'Jack Robinson.' Fainted, I guess. Lord! It was quick. Quickest thing I ever saw in all my life."

"It's impossible, I tell you! Absolutely impossible!"

It was Brian who spoke in that frenzied hoarse voice, which Irene had never heard before. Her knees quaked under her.

Dave Freeland said: "Just a minute, Brian. Irene was there beside her. Let's hear what she has to say."

She had a moment of stark craven fear. "Oh God," she thought, prayed, "help me."

A strange man, official and authoritative, addressed her. "You're sure she fell? Her husband didn't give her a shove or anything like that, as Dr. Redfield seems to think?"

For the first time she was aware that Bellew was not in the little group shivering in the small hallway. What did that mean? As she began to work it out in her numbed mind, she was shaken with another hideous trembling. Not that! Oh, not that!

"No, no!" she protested. "I'm quite certain that he didn't. I was there, too. As close as he was. She just fell, before anybody could stop her. I—"

Her quaking knees gave way under her. She

moaned and sank down, moaned again. Through the great heaviness that submerged and drowned her she was dimly conscious of strong arms lifting her up. Then everything was dark.

Centuries after, she heard the strange man saying: "Death by misadventure, I'm inclined to believe. Let's go up and have another look at that window."[3]

NOTES

DEDICATION

1. *For Carl Van Vechten and Fania Marinoff:* Larsen's dedication acknowledged her friends and supporters Carl Van
   Vechten (1886–1964) and his wife, Fania Marinoff
   (1887–1972). Novelist, photographer, and music and
   drama critic, Van Vechten was a patron of the arts and
   black artists during the Harlem Renaissance. Author of
   the controversial novel *Nigger Heaven* (1926), he was also
   a bohemian bon vivant and habitué of Harlem's exotic
   nightlife. He and his wife were widely known for their
   lavish interracial parties downtown, and acted as a kind
   of bridge between the Harlem Renaissance artists and
   their white publishers and promoters. It was Van
   Vechten who recommended Larsen's work—along with

that of James Weldon Johnson, Langston Hughes, and Rudolph Fisher—to Knopf, his own publisher.

EPIGRAPH

1. *One three centuries removed ... What is Africa to me?:* The novel's epigraph is from Countee Cullen's famous poem "Heritage," from his first published volume of poetry, *Color* (1925). Cullen (1903–1946) was the most celebrated poet among the New Negro writers and is known for his lyricism. He was widely acclaimed for his Keatsian sonnet "Yet Do I Marvel," which concludes with the lines, "Yet do I marvel at this curious thing / To make a poet black, and bid him sing." He was also chided by some of his contemporaries for making the statement, "If I am going to be a poet at all, I am going to be a POET and not [a] NEGRO POET." One thus notes with some irony that his best-known poems address issues of race.

PART ONE: ENCOUNTER

CHAPTER TWO

1. *Samaritan:* as in the "good Samaritan" (Luke 10:30–37); one who is compassionate and helpful to those in distress.

2. *finger-nails ... silly rot:* During the 1920s, the popular press teemed with warnings about those with "Negro

blood" sliding quietly into the ranks of whiteness and offered several physical characteristics—among them the presence of a particularly distinct half moon or a dark blue tint on the fingernails, a clear difference in pigmentation between the palm and the back of the hand, and other "subtle" physical markers—as a litmus test of hidden African ancestry. Nearly every state in the union had some version of the one-drop rule, conceived during slavery, that held an individual legally black at the presence of a single drop of Negro blood. These physical markers—and by extension the one-drop rule—are the targets of Irene's derision and derive from the widely accepted "principles" of the Victorian pseudosciences of the late nineteenth century. The Victorians in both England and the United States were awash in race theories and phrenology, pseudosciences that found their clearest expression in eugenics, a theory—and later practice—founded by Charles Darwin's cousin Francis Galton (1822–1911) in the mid-nineteenth century that applied horse-breeding principles to human reproduction.

3. *"Marshall Field's":* Marshall Field and Company remains Chicago's largest retail department store. Established in 1852, its renovation (after the great fire of 1871) installed a neoclassical design that suggested not only its dominance in the world of modern retail sales but also its cultural authority as an arbiter of fashion and taste

for the affluent. Although the store also served a less-affluent clientele in the 1920s, it catered primarily to a wealthy elite class. Shopping at Marshall Field's thus reaffirmed the social standing and cultural taste of its white patrons. Clare's shopping at such an establishment would have suggested her desire for race privilege and class status, and their material accouterments. Except for this reference and the one that follows, these explanatory notes do not highlight Larsen's numerous references to the urban geography of Chicago, as they simply serve to locate the novel's action. For more on these geographical references, see the notes in Thadious Davis's edition of *Passing* (Penguin, 1997).

4. *"Idlewild"*: an African-American vacation resort located in Manistee National Forest, Lake County, Michigan. It was popular for its lakeside beach, horseback riding, hunting, and other amusements during the 1920s and well into the twentieth century. Frequented by affluent blacks, Idlewild was for the black Midwest what Oak Bluffs on Martha's Vineyard was for the black elite in the Northeast. See Robert Stepto's "[F]rom Idlewild and Other Seasons" (*Callaloo* 14:1 [1991], pp. 20–36).

5. *"Negro blood"*: refers to black ancestry and is part of a pseudoscientific discourse predicated on the notion that race was biologically defined. "Negro blood" was thus conceived of as different from "white blood," and in the instance of miscegenation would "stain" the "purity" of

the "white" bloodline. In the West Indies, some whites claimed that the Negro's blood was indeed "black." Notably, this discourse references the white perspective; black discourse might refer to "white blood."

6. *"sons and daughters of Ham"*: reference to Ham, father of Canaan, and his descendants, the Canaanites (Genesis 9:20–27). According to the Bible, the progeny of Noah's three sons, Shem, Ham, and Japheth, populated the earth after the flood. When Noah became drunk from the wine of his vineyard and lay uncovered within his tent, he was gazed upon and mocked by his son Ham, who went and told his brothers that their father lay naked. When Noah awoke and discovered what Ham had done, he cursed his progeny, "Cursed be Canaan; a servant of servants shall he be unto his brethren." This biblical passage was often invoked by proslavery advocates to provide scriptural justification for the enslavement of Africans in the American South.

7. *"the tar-brush"*: slang (disparaging and offensive) for black ancestry—as in brushed or "painted" with tar. Among whites, the term was used to refer to someone "black" who may not actually be so; among African Americans, the term may also refer to dark-skinned blacks.

CHAPTER THREE

1. *"I nearly died of terror ... for fear that she might be dark"*: Clare expresses fear of the consequences of reproduc-

tion and racial passing, namely, the popular belief that "race will out." The discourse on color between Clare and Gertrude expresses the anxiety of the passer that, despite skipping generations, the grosser anatomical features of race will eventually resurface, either in the first-generation offspring of miscegenated unions or in subsequent generations. The white counterpart of such a conviction would be "there's a nigger in the wood-pile," meaning that black ancestry will sooner or later manifest itself. Such a discourse represents the fear or conviction of the "return of the repressed" at the level of the body. Interestingly, such folk convictions may have been supported at the scientific level by the findings of such nineteenth-century investigators as biologist and botanist Gregor Johann Mendel (1822–1884), whose experiments with plants led to the formulation of the principles of heredity that provided the basis for modern genetics. Furthermore, the legal doctrine of the one-drop rule both drew on and contributed to these popular notions. Also, it is clear that here Larsen expresses the anxiety and frustration associated with her own status as the visibly black child of "white" parents. See Thadious Davis's biography, *Nella Larsen, Novelist of the Harlem Renaissance* (Louisiana State University Press, 1994).

2. *"A black Jew"*: most likely pertaining to or derived from the Abyssinian, or Ethiopian, Jews (as opposed to the

Semitic Jews). Black Jews consider themselves one of the lost tribes of Israel and descendants of the first Jews, who, they believe, originated in Abyssinia, or Ethiopia. Interestingly, modern DNA research has proved that the Lemba, a group of black Jews in southern Africa who have long claimed priestly lineage, share the Y chromosome of the Cohanim, the Semitic priestly line traced back to Aaron. These genetic results have given credence to claims of an ancestral Jewish link for black Jews. More problematic are those whose link to Judaism is not clearly genetic. The Church of God in Philadelphia, for example, founded by Prophet F. S. Cherry, believes that Christ, with his "lamb's wool hair," was black. Current followers of Prophet Cherry consider themselves black Jews. One of the earliest studies of black Jews in America, based in part on Cherry's followers, is a chapter in Arthur Huff Fauset's *Black Gods of the Metropolis* (University of Pennsylvania Press, 1944); some recent scholars have argued that Fauset (and others who study black Jews in the United States) use vague, often nonracial definitions of Judaism that hopelessly skew their results. Larsen may also be referring more specifically to the Jewish congregations founded in Harlem by Chief Rabbi Wentworth Arthur Matthew (1892–1973) and his rabbinical students, beginning in 1919. Rabbi Matthew was closely connected to Marcus Garvey's Universal Negro Improvement Association

(UNIA) by way of Rabbi Arnold J. Ford, the group's musical director.

3. *wartime in France ... the new gaiety of Budapest:* Clare's travels take her through France, Germany, England, and Austria-Hungary during World War I (1914–1918) and its aftermath (1919–1926). *After-the-wartime in Germany* refers to the Weimar Republic. At the time *Passing* takes place, Germany was a country of contrasts. Just beneath the gaiety and extravagance of the wild, opulent cabaret scene of Berlin was the crushing poverty of the failing German economy, which was, b y the late 1920s, careening toward collapse under the weight of the war reparations imposed on Germany by the Treaty of Versailles at the Paris Peace Conference in 1919. Adolf Hitler's National Socialists had also taken root: Hitler had founded the Schutzstaffel (S.S.) and published his manifesto, *Mein Kampf,* in 1925. Within five years of *Passing*'s publication, President Paul von Hindenburg (elected president of the Weimar Republic in 1925) would name Hitler chancellor, paving the way for Hitler's ascension to power in 1934. The *general strike* refers to the striking coal miners in England who requested the Trades Union Congress (TUC) to convene a general strike in sympathy in early May 1925. More than two and a half million workers in transport, newspapers, and the iron and steel industries participated in the strike, which lasted for nine days. In response, the

British government deployed troops to control essential supplies under the Emergency Powers Act of 1920. Although the TUC called off the strike, the miners did not return to work until November 1925. The *dressmakers' openings in Paris* refers to the Art Deco exposition that opened in Paris in July 1925, showcasing clothes, jewelry, and other decorative arts, providing a stimulus to the Parisian houses of high fashion. Designers such as Poiret, Chanel, Vionnet, Lanvin, Babani, Worth, and others secured Paris's status as the center of fashion in the 1920s (see note for page 141, page 198). *The new gaiety of Budapest:* The period between World War I and World War II, particularly the 1920s, is often referred to as the Silver Age of Budapest. During this time, the city was part of the Grand Tour, known for its spas and casinos that attracted Europe's wealthy elite; the novelist Evelyn Waugh and the Prince of Wales were among its frequent visitors.

4. *And something else for which she could find no name:* a line suggestively reminiscent of the phrase associated with Oscar Wilde, "the love that dare not speak its name," referring to homosexual love. In a November 12, 1930, letter to Carl Van Vechten, Larsen writes that upon meeting a haughty Englishman (whose name was apparently Douglas), she quipped, "Pardon me, but are you the Lord Douglas who slept with Oscar Wilde?" (quoted in Thadious Davis's *Nella Larsen, Novelist of the*

Harlem Renaissance [Louisiana State University Press, 1994], p. 11). Though often associated with Wilde, the original phrase is from a sonnet, "The Two Loves," by Wilde's "lover-in-disgrace," Lord Alfred Douglas. I am indebted to my friend and colleague Chip Delany for this clarification. Although critics have failed to note it, this line further underscores the homoerotic subtext of Larsen's novel.

PART TWO: RE-ENCOUNTER

CHAPTER ONE

1. *sardony:* Apparently, this is Larsen's neologism linking the adjective *sardonic* with the noun *irony,* suggesting a mix of surprise and bitter humor, which is character- ized by scorn, mockery, derision, and a reversal of ex- pectation.

2. *"Seventh Avenue, and Lenox Avenue":* The area to which Brian refers was the heart of Prohibition Harlem, the speakeasy district bounded by 125th and 135th streets and by Lenox and Seventh avenues in the years be- tween 1920 and 1933. Among the vast array of speakeasies, lounges, cafes, supper clubs, theaters, ball- rooms, and dance halls, one could find the famous Cot- ton Club (Lenox and 125th) and the Hurtig and Seamon's Burlesque, which in 1934 became the Apollo Theater. Nearly all these establishments were segre-

gated; though always featuring black entertainers, these establishments were open to black patrons only after the white crowds had gone home. Of the theaters, for example, only the Alhambra and the Crescent were "black," while the Cotton Club and Connie's Inn were "whites only" (together with Small's Paradise and Barron Wilkins's Club, these comprised the "big four"). At the time Larsen's novel takes place, this area of Harlem is in its heyday, the golden age of Harlem nightlife. And as Brian's not so subtle suggestion indicates, the Lenox–Seventh Avenue area was a site of illicit and illegal (and racially charged) recreation.

3. *"shine":* disparaging term for a black male, as in the various toasts on "Shine and the *Titanic."* The term is most likely derived from *shoeshine boy* and the shine or blackening associated with the surface of polished shoes.

4. *"sheba":* slang term for an attractive black woman; probably signifying on the African Queen of Sheba, who, according to the Old Testament, is associated with wealth and great beauty. Possibly related to—although not necessarily the counterpart of—*sheik,* a popular epithet for a black lover or gigolo (or one who dresses like one), most likely popularized by its association with romantic screen idol Rudolph Valentino (1895–1926) for his signature roles, *The Sheik* (1921) and *Son of the Sheik* (1926).

5. *"Instinct of the race to survive and expand":* notion associ-

ated with Charles Darwin (1809–1882) and the theory of organic evolution advanced in *Origin of Species* (1859) and *The Descent of Man* (1871). In his "principle of natural selection," Darwin promoted the idea that organisms are competitive and result in the survival of the fittest variant.

CHAPTER TWO

1. *"Mr. Wentworth"*: Hugh and Bianca Wentworth are modeled on Carl Van Vechten and Fania Marinoff (see note for Dedication, page 183).
2. *"the Negro Welfare League"*: Larsen's parodic equivalent of the Negro uplift organizations that worked on behalf of racial progress and advancement. Best known among such organizations were the National Association for the Advancement of Colored People (NAACP) and the Urban League.
3. *"shekels"*: slang term for cash, money; originally the chief silver coin of the ancient Hebrews (and currently a monetary unit in Israel).

CHAPTER THREE

1. *"Rich man, poor man"*: popular children's nursery rhyme.
2. *"Nordic"*: slang for white, a term in currency among blacks and whites during the period; originally of or pertaining to Germanic people of northern European

origin, exemplified by the Scandinavians, or having physical characteristics (e.g., blond hair, blue eyes) associated with northern Europeans. Given her Scandinavian background, such a term would have had an especially fraught meaning for Larsen.

3. *"'butter and egg' men"*: Here used derisively, this refers to farmers or small-town businessmen who spend money extravagantly when they come to the big city. A popular 1927 song, "The Big Butter and Egg Man," made the "big butter and egg man from the West" synonymous with the sucker or free-spender. Texas Guinan, a New York City nightclub entertainer, popularized the description of her best customers as "big butter and egg men" with that song (see Lax and Smith, *The Great Song Thesaurus*). I'm indebted to Connie Eble, editor of *American Speech*, for help in tracking down this elusive term.

4. *"Terpsichorean art"*: pertaining to dance, especially social dance. In classical mythology, Terpsichore was the Muse of dance.

5. *"dicty"*: Harlemese for a "swell" or "high-toned" person, meaning snobbish, pretentious, haughty, or "hinckty," often referring to the black bourgeoisie or "upper-class"; opposite of *rat*, meaning lower-class; I would guess that the more recent term *siddity* (or *s'ditty*) represents a contraction of *so-dicty*—a term that used to be applied to black women who were considered to

be "putting on airs," especially with speech, or trying to act more sophisticated than seemed warranted by their class background.

6. "*fay*'": Harlemese slang for a white person, seemingly derived from pig Latin for *foe;* cryptic racial code intended to confuse white people. Rudolph Fisher, Harlem Renaissance novelist, defines *ofay* as a contraction of *old* and *fay,* which is the original term. The term is the literary predecessor of *honkey* and *whitey.*

7. "*Slippin' me, Irene?*": to dodge or evade, as in "to give one the slip" or to equivocate; also to trick or "put one over" on someone; possibly related to the later term *slipping and sliding,* which means "two-timing."

PART THREE: FINALE

CHAPTER ONE

1. "*Josephine Baker*": Baker (1906–1975) was the toast of Paris in the 1920s. She made her Parisian debut in 1925 in *La Revue Nègre* at the Théâtre des Champs-Élysées and later became the star of the Folies-Bergère. She embodied for the French the essence of exotic primitivism. Notably, Baker did not appear in *Shuffle Along* (see note below) when she auditioned for its Philadelphia opening, because (as Baker claimed) she was considered "too dark" to be a chorine. In New York, where it became a great hit, Baker again auditioned for *Shuffle*

Along and was placed as the "end girl" in the chorus line. Because of her talent, Noble Sissle and Eubie Blake also created a special part for her as a comedienne in the chorus line of *The Chocolate Dandies* (1924).

2. "Shuffle Along": black musical comedy that became a smash Broadway hit in 1921, where it ran for over five hundred performances. It was composed by Eubie Blake (1883–1983) and Noble Sissle (1889–1975), and written by Aubrey Lyles (1882–1932) and Flournoy Miller (1889–1971). This show introduced the black musical review to Broadway, and paved the way for later popular shows, including *The Chocolate Dandies* and *Keep Shufflin'*.

3. *"Ethel Waters"*: Waters (1896–1977) was a talented blues, jazz, and, later, gospel singer, as well as a dramatic actress, who began her career on the vaudeville circuit, where she was known as "Sweet Mama Stringbean." She later received critical acclaim as a nightclub performer, Broadway star, and recording artist during the 1920s. Recording on the Black Swan and Columbia labels, she was especially popular for her recordings of "Dinah" (1925) and "Stormy Weather" (1933). Unlike many entertainers, her career survived the Harlem Renaissance, and she became best known for performances in DuBose Heyward's *Mamba's Daughters* (1939) and *Cabin in the Sky* (1940), and Carson McCullers's *The Member of the Wedding* (1950). She was also nominated for an Acad-

emy Award as Best Supporting Actress for her role in *Pinky* (1949), a film about racial passing.

4. *"Worth ... Lanvin ... Babani":* Charles Frederick Worth, Jeanne Lanvin, and Babani were all well-known designers associated with the great houses of haute couture in Paris during the early twentieth century. Worth opened the first fashion house in Paris and pioneered the look that became the prototype for women's tailored suits; Lanvin's most successful designs were her low-cut and low-waisted, ankle-length Basque dresses, or *robes de style;* Babani's fashions were made from unusual fabrics and often featured unique details, such as corded tassels and metallic embroidery.

5. *Dave Freeland:* Larsen's biographer, Thadious Davis, correctly suggests that this character is modeled on novelist and short-story writer Rudolph "Bud" Fisher (1897–1934). His first novel, *The Walls of Jericho,* was published in 1928, the same year as Larsen's first novel, *Quicksand.*

6. *"subway ... underground":* The direct reference here is to the Underground Railroad, the loose network of safe houses and routes north through which escaping slaves passed from the early days of the Colonies until the early days of the Civil War. Between the American Revolution and the mid-nineteenth century, in fact, perhaps as many as 100,000 slaves escaped to freedom. The connection of the Underground Railroad to the

abolitionist movement after 1800 underscores its inherently revolutionary and transgressive effects. It is to these effects that Irene somewhat ironically—and also ambiguously—refers in her "history" of the once-Confederate cup's journey north (the implication is perhaps that the cup is "stolen property" since recovered) and in her tongue-in-cheek recounting of the cup's untimely demise just moments earlier. In light of Irene's tangled relationship to her own passing, her barbed synonyms for the Underground Railroad—the urban (and thus quintessentially New York) *subway* and the English (read pretentious) *underground*—play nicely on her own complicated and subterranean racial (and arguably, sexual) identity.

CHAPTER TWO

1. *He slept in his room next to hers at night:* It was not unusual for husbands and wives, especially upper- and upper-middle-class couples, to maintain separate bedrooms, or even separate apartments. Socially, this arrangement would have served as a marker of status: only wealth allowed space enough for separate accommodations.

2. *Ham's dark children:* According to the Bible, after the flood, Noah's sons—Shem, Ham, Japheth—populated the earth. Shem's descendants became the Semites, from whom the Hebrews and most of the Middle Eastern peoples were descended; Ham's descendants be-

came the Hamites, and the peoples of North Africa; and
Japheth's descendants became the Ethiopians and
Egyptians, many of whom migrated northward into Europe and Asia. As Noah's second—and accursed—son,
as well as the father of Canaan (see note for page 33 on
page 187), Ham would have become the ancestor and
progenitor of the usually dark-skinned peoples of
North and East Africa, and Mesopotamia, including
Ethiopians, Egyptians, Berbers, Babylonians, etc. Recent scholarship has both promoted and contested the
"Hamitic hypothesis," which challenges the assumption
that the origins and predominant culture of ancient
Egypt was Semitic. Other scholars challenge the attempt to distinguish between so-called Hamitic (Euro-
African and Mediterranean) and more phenotypically
black or Negroid racial classifications.

CHAPTER THREE

1. *the Avenue:* Fifth Avenue, in Manhattan. In midtown,
   from 34th to 59th streets, Fifth Avenue is known for its
   fashionable department stores and stylish boutiques.
2. *mashers:* A masher is a man who makes sexual advances,
   especially to women he does not know; a flirt.
3. *"queered":* spoiled or ruined; put into a disadvantageous
   situation. Larsen's repeated use of *queer* as an adjectival
   synonym for "strange" or "unusual" is curious, given the
   term's widespread use at the time of Larsen's writing as

slang for homosexual. The added connotations of its use as a verb in this instance to suggest "ruin" or "spoilage" perhaps echo the word's slang meaning, not only to the contemporary reader but perhaps even to the original readers of *Passing*. See Deborah McDowell's introduction to *Passing and Quicksand* (Rutgers University Press, 1986) for an extended reading of the lesbian subtext of Larsen's novel.

4. *"gone native"*: a reversal of the original meaning of this phrase, in which someone civilized, presumably white, "regresses" to a "native," or savage, state. In Larsen's reversal, *gone native* is a synonym for passing, a play on the idea of blending into the "native" white surroundings. For more on this reversed sense of the phrase, see Marianna Torgovnick's *Gone Primitive: Savage Intellect, Modern Lives* (University of Chicago Press, 1990).

5. *the Rhinelander case:* This was a highly publicized court case that involved the marriage of Leonard Kip Rhinelander, a member of a wealthy and aristocratic New York clan, and Alice B. Jones, a mulatto chambermaid in his household. Married on October 14, 1924, Leonard filed for an annulment after the first month, on the grounds that Jones had fraudulently entered the marriage by falsifying her racial identity. After her lawyers first claimed that she was white, Alice Rhinelander filed a countersuit in which she charged that her husband knew her true racial status (she was a

quadroon, a person of one-quarter black ancestry) before their marriage and that he had ardently pursued
her nonetheless. As the trial proceeded, Leonard con-
fessed with some embarrassment that indeed he did
know that she was a mulatto before marriage but that
his father had strongly objected to Alice's black ancestry. During the course of the trial, the white newspapers
sensationalized the proceedings (the black newspapers
less so), and Leonard's love letters were read in open
court, while Alice was forced to partially disrobe so that
the jury could examine her skin color. On December 5,
1925, the jury rendered its verdict (in spite of the racist
closing argument of the prosecution), exonerating
Alice from charges of fraud. Leonard's attempts to appeal the verdict would prove costly and futile. In 1927
(the temporal setting of *Passing*), Alice filed a suit for
separation on the grounds of abandonment as well as
"cruel and inhuman treatment" as a consequence of the
trial publicity. When a divorce decree was granted, in
1930, Alice received a cash settlement of $31,500 (her
husband had spent more than $50,000 in legal fees),
along with a quarterly annuity of $3,600, payable for
the rest of her life. Six years later, at age thirty-four,
Leonard died of pneumonia. For further details of the
case and its significance for Larsen, see Mark J. Madigan's "Miscegenation and 'The Dicta of Race and

Class': The Rhinelander Case and Nella Larsen's *Passing*" (*Modern Fiction Studies* 36:4 [Winter 1990]).

CHAPTER FOUR

1. *"C.P. time":* colored people's time; used jocularly in the African-American vernacular to mean late, lagging, or behind the appointed time; opposite of punctual or "on time."

2. *"nigger-power":* walking; the term suggests a forerunner of "black power" but without the ideological or political connotations. It refers to the achievement of a task by virtue of brute strength and endurance, rather than by ancillary (or machine) power. A legendary example might be John Henry, the "steel-drivin' man."

3. *Centuries after ...:* Two different endings to the novel were published by Alfred A. Knopf in 1929. The first and second printings concluded with the following paragraph:

> Centuries after, she heard the strange man saying, "Death by misadventure, I'm inclined to believe. Let's go up and have another look at that window."

The third printing, however, omits this passage, concluding with "Then everything was dark." Later editions, including those published by The Arno Press (1969), Negro Universities Press (1969), Ayer Publishing Company (1985), and Rutgers University Press (1986), close with the abridged version. In contrast, the 1971 Collier Books edition (Macmillan) and the 1997 Penguin Books edition conclude with the extended ending. The Modern Library edition also contains the original extended ending. Interestingly, editor Deborah McDowell states in her introduction to the Rutgers edition that "[t]his closing paragraph does not seem to alter the spirit of the original in any way." I am inclined to believe that the ending does makes a difference, in that the amended conclusion enhances its status as a "writerly" text—in the sense that French critic Roland Barthes defines as "writerly" an open-ended text that requires the reader to collaborate in producing its meaning.

READING GROUP GUIDE

1. *Passing* is set in the 1920s, before the Supreme Court declared "separate but equal" facilities for nonwhites unconstitutional. What privileges are Irene Redfield denied as a black person? What do men and women gain by passing?

2. In Part One, Irene has tea with Gertrude and Clare, her two childhood friends. Compare the attitudes each woman has toward passing. To what degree does each pass for white?

3. *Passing* presents two women, Irene Redfield and Clare Kendry, who make very different choices yet whose lives intertwine in startling ways. Compare the charac-

ters of each. What are each woman's strengths? Her weaknesses? What are each woman's attitudes toward race? How do these attitudes influence the novel's plot?

4. Consider Irene's fear that Brian and Clare may be having an affair. Does her anxiety seem reasonable to you? Why, or why not?

5. Compare different characters' attitudes toward sexuality. For instance, in what ways are Irene's and Clare's thoughts on sex similar? How are they different? How might these attitudes be related to each character's thoughts on race?

6. Discuss the novel's ending. Do you think Irene pushed Clare? What evidence does the novel offer either for or against this interpretation?

7. Certain critics have suggested that an erotic attachment exists between Irene and Clare. Do you agree with this reading? What evidence can you find in the novel to support this idea?